TROPICAL ❧ FISH

TROPICAL FISH

Tales from Entebbe

DOREEN BAINGANA

Harlem Moon
Broadway Books
New York

Published by Harlem Moon, an imprint of Broadway Books, a division of
Random House, Inc.

A previous edition of this book was originally published in 2005 by University
of Massachusetts Press.

Reading Group Companion by P. Llanor Alleyne

Visit our website at www.harlemmoon.com

Book design by Claire Vaccaro

Library of Congress Cataloging-in-Publication Data
Baingana, Doreen.
Tropical fish : tales from Entebbe / by Doreen Baingana.—1st ed.
p. cm.
Contents: Green stones—Hunger—First kiss—Passion—A thank-you note—
Tropical fish—Lost in Los Angeles—Questions of home.
1. Entebbe (Uganda)—Fiction. 2. Uganda—Social life and customs—Fiction.
I. Title.

PR9402.9.B35T76 2006
823'.92—dc22
2005046770

ISBN 0-7679-2510-6

PRINTED IN THE UNITED STATES OF AMERICA

10 9 8 7 6 5 4 3 2 1

First Harlem Moon Edition

To

Gladys Kebirungi Baingana Tabaro

who thrilled us into reading

CONTENTS

It has been about three years since I finished *Tropical Fish,* and since then I have been asked what inspired me to write this work of fiction, whether it is autobiographical or not, and what its political and social context is. I hope my answers here do not overinfluence the reader's engagement with the stories. I believe that once a writer has sent her work out into the world, it takes on a life of its own. The writer should let go. The work becomes what each reader perceives it to be, irrespective of the author's intentions, including those I express here.

All but one of the tales are set in Uganda, a small, landlocked country in Eastern Africa that has had a turbulent history since its independence in 1962. The novel occurs during the aftermath of the military regime of the notorious president Idi Amin, who ruled from 1971 to 1979. He led by decree, ordering summary executions of his enemies and mandating laws bent on destroying civil society. His unruly army was left free to murder, torture, rob, and in other ways terrorize the population, which pushed many into exile.

One of Amin's most despicable acts was to give the Ugandan Asian community seventy-two hours to leave the country in 1972. The Indians had lived in the country for more than three generations and were the backbone of the economy. This rash and inhumane move led to the almost total collapse of the economy, which was made worse by international sanctions. The result was extreme deprivation at all levels, including major shortages of basic goods such as sugar, salt, and medical supplies. Only the black market thrived. The situation remained almost the same in the early eighties through numerous regime changes. As the political climate stabilized in the late eighties, however, Uganda was hit by another catastrophe: HIV/AIDS. Yet again, we were completely at the mercy of an immense force, a hurricane, a plague.

Apart from HIV/AIDS, I do not deal directly with the other disasters. Rather, they are a backdrop for the story of three sisters taking separate and distinct journeys of self-discovery. I was interested not merely in depicting the horror but in exploring what kinds of lives, interior and otherwise, were created amid or despite the difficult circumstances beyond the issue of survival. I, not always deliberately, posed certain questions and suggested possible answers. What, for urban Ugandan girls and young women, is normal? How and why do individuals who start out in the same milieu make different choices and thus follow different destinies? My girls navigate family love in all its imperfection, fall in love, take up religion or rebellion, and chase their curiosity and need as far as they can take them, whether to foreign shores, a dead end, or deeper inside themselves.

Fiction provides personalized takes on universal questions. It does not provide The Answer, since it does not exist. This work, therefore, should not be read as representations of African womanhood but as possibilities, instances, imaginings. And, no, it is not an autobiography. Rather, I used some of my experiences and observations as clay, added all kinds of water and paint, and shaped and molded this into varied pots: these stories. I aim for the "emotional truth," that element that makes fiction ring true and carry meaning. The stories are linked like sisters, forming a family that is stronger than its individual parts.

I hope that reading *Tropical Fish* is as much a journey of discovery for the reader as it was for me to write it.

—Doreen Baingana,
January 2006, Entebbe, Uganda

ACKNOWLEDGMENTS

Some of these stories originally appeared, in slightly different form, in the following journals.

"Green Stones" in *Chelsea* 73 (May 2003)
"Hunger" in *The Sun,* no. 327 (March 2003)
"First Kiss" in *Meridian,* no. 10 (Fall/Winter 2002)
"Tropical Fish" in *African American Review* 37, no. 4 (Winter 2002)
"Lost in Los Angeles" in *Glimmer Train,* no. 48 (Fall 2003)
"Questions of Home" in *Callaloo* 27, no. 2 (Spring 2004)

I am deeply grateful to the University of Maryland Creative Writing Program for giving me the time and space to write, and to my teachers Joyce Kornblatt, Merle Collins, John Auchard, and Howard Norman for their excellent guidance. Special thanks to Do Hee Kim and Steven Thomas, and to my inspiring sisters-in-writing, Stephanie Allen, Angel Threatt, and Donna Hemans, for their friendship and great advice. Thanks also to Douglas Mpuga, who edited the Luganda and Runyankore phrases, my editors Amanda Heller and Carol Betsch, and my agent, Christina Ward. I am most grateful to E. Ethelbert Miller for encouraging me early on.

Much thanks to the Association of Writers and Writing Programs, the District of Columbia Commission on the Arts and Humanities for an Artist's Grant, and the Special English Department of the Voice of America for keeping a roof over my head.

I could not have done this without the support of my family and friends in the United States and Uganda (you know who you are), especially my sister Florence Baingana. Thank you.

Abagyenda bareeba.

Those who travel, see.

·KINYANKORE PROVERB·

TROPICAL ❀ FISH

i

Green Stones

I was once a child, growing up in Entebbe, spending most of my time with Rusi, the housegirl, especially during the holidays, while my older sisters were away at boarding school. I followed Rusi around the house in the mornings as she cleaned up. It was a fun way to idle away the time. Rusi talked incessantly to herself or to whoever was around. She spoke Luganda only. She complained that I disturbed her, didn't help at all, that I just followed her around like an irritating little dog. Couldn't I find something useful to do, she would moan. Oh, when would school start again so she could have her quiet house back. I spoiled everything. Don't touch that, or that, she yelled, as if the clothes or plates or pictures were hers. You'll break it, you little rat! She'd swipe at my bare feet with a broom or bedsheet, which I'd dodge, giggling, and continue to follow her through the house.

The room I loved most was my mother and father's bedroom, mostly because we were not allowed into it. The room was kept dim, its thick curtains patterned with blood-red roses closed to keep the heat out. This red glow added to its sacredness, as if it were a quiet, empty cathedral or mysterious fortune-teller's den.

At night in bed, sucking my thumb furiously, I went over imaginary fears; they were an irresistible itch I scratched again and again. What if I was caught sneaking around the forbidden room opening drawers, reading letters, sniffing the faint mysterious smells of Maama and Taata; cigarettes, polish, powder, perfume, sweat, and more? I imagined suddenly hearing Taata's heavy ringing footsteps. They got louder as he came down the corridor. I was trapped! I froze, then as I hastened to hide, tripped over a chair and fell. Down crashed the wooden chair right on top of me. Maama's bright jewelry flew out of my hands and colored the air like fat butterflies, before cascading down and shattering repeatedly, spreading tiny cutting shards all over the floor. Precious beads rolled under the wide bed, joining lost brushes, coins, and dust, never to be found again. The door creaked open . . . delicious terror. Why did I dread and dream about this? Why did I fear Taata?

When Rusi bustled in to clean my parents' room, however, with me trailing behind her, the room became ordinary. Rusi pushed the huge mound of her breasts like pillows ahead of her as she energetically marched in. She pulled back the thick curtains and flung open the windows to the startling sunshine outside, the squawk and trill of birds, the shouts and the escape of raggedy kids surprised to be seen stealing mangoes from the tree nearest my parents' bedroom. With Rusi there and the dark red glow gone, the solemn church became a rowdy marketplace. My parents' huge throne of a bed, still unmade, was just a bed, ruffled and somehow smaller. Sprinklings of dust floated in the sunlight as Rusi shook out the sheets and dusted the coffee-colored bedside tables and mirror. Her talk and laughter filled the air, offending me. Had she no sense of the room's sacredness? But when I lay down on my parents' bed, Rusi chased me off with a wild swing that was meant to miss. I couldn't help laughing at her flabby underarms flapping like wings.

Rusi was easy to laugh at. I teased her about the neighbor's *shamba-boy*, Paulo, who bought her a hand mirror, gave her old calendar pictures, and even a pair of shoes. He used a mirror himself every morning, right outside his one-window boys' quarters. His daily ritual was to wet, oil, comb, and pat his hair into shape. He combed and patted, combed and patted, admired the round Afro shape from all sides, and then came to the kitchen door to ask Rusi for tea and her time. She didn't get angry when I teased her; rather, she called Paulo a fool and joked about his big head and floppy ears, then joined me in laughter.

Rusi's laugh was special, a spectacular performance. First a grunt, deep in her chest, *ggrrumph*, as if she was mad about something, then a louder guffaw, once, paced out. More silence as she gathered her breath and energy, grimacing as though she had a bellyache, as if the joke was killing her, and then, just when you thought it wasn't going to happen this time, she really was mad, the volcano erupted, the tornado, the hurricane! There was nothing else to do but giggle as I watched her with awe and some apprehension. What if she choked? But no, she moved through louder, shriller laughing stages. She couldn't be stopped or helped.

Any word would send her deeper into the vortex of sound and painful glee as she clutched her trembling breasts, bent over like an old woman, held her back for support, roaring, then bent backwards, her breasts reaching up into the air—you just had to laugh in applause. Finally, she would wipe tears off her face, sighing, *eeh-eh, ahhhh, Katonda wange! My God!* to calm herself down. When she turned back to her broom, dust cloth, or washing, I felt I had been through a religious experience and had landed exhausted, but safe and sane, on the other side.

Once Rusi recovered and was back at work I had to stop giggling, or she would turn on me sternly. "Are you laughing at me? Who are you laughing with? Not me, for sure, get out, *ggenda!* Let me work, take your teeth somewhere else," she'd grumble, as she swept me furiously out of the room. Her mirth left her joyless, angry almost, as if she had exhausted all her resources of humor.

Much as I loved Rusi's company, after lunch was my time alone, in the heavy heat of the afternoon, when the only sound was the droning of a bumblebee caught in a window net somewhere. I was supposed to sleep off my lunch after Maama and Taata returned to work. Rusi cleared up the meal and left dishes sparkling with clean water in the kitchen, then she too went to her room in the boys' quarters at the back of our compound. I lay in bed rereading the adventure stories of Enid Blyton or the Narnia books until all was quiet, then crept off for my own adventure.

My parents' door always creaked open, as if there was someone calling me in, another naughty child like me, my invisible counterpart in the netherworld. Yet again, to my surprise, the glowing, mysterious room was real. The rosy air was thick with secrets. This forever twilight, hidden from the hard stare of the afternoon sun outside, was a presence I breathed in deeply. Ah, those silent, hazy afternoons, when even the birds took a siesta; it was too hot to flit around squealing and trilling. The silence became louder as another heavy, buzzing bluebottle fly knocked itself senseless behind the blood-red curtains, trapped blindly between glass and net.

I left the door slightly ajar to clearly see Maama's forbidden treasure. In the dim light two tall mahogany wardrobes looked like huge dark priests silently disapproving of me. Luckily, they were too fat to move, so I stuck out my tongue at them. There! Up on the wall above the bed was a photograph of my father's parents, but I wasn't scared of them either; they were much too old to count. Still, just in case, I greeted them silently in Runyankore: *Agandi, basebo.* Taata's mother, Omukikuru, was still alive, but lived far away in the village, Rusozi, so she wouldn't know what I was up to. She never smiled, and when she visited, which was rare, thank God, she refused to eat Rusi's food because she is a Muganda. Maama had to leave work early and cook special dishes for her: black beans prepared with ghee, or steamed *biringanya.* Despite Maama's efforts, Omukikuru's mouth got tighter and tighter with disapproval. I really didn't like it when she visited.

Taata's father died long before I was born. He had the fiercest face I had ever seen, possibly because of a life spent with my grandmother. In the photo, his face was wrinkled into a tight scrawl. He held his *kanzu* firmly straight down with huge hands wound over and over with prominent veins. Was his *kanzu* about to spring open and show his legs? I covered my giggle with my hand because even I knew one shouldn't laugh at the dead, especially at your own relatives, who are looking out for you. But I did every time, and so far nothing had happened. Maama said such things are true only if you believed them, so I didn't. The same with *juju*, which I did want to believe in sometimes, especially when a school friend dropped me for someone else, or a teacher mocked me before the whole class.

Even after my respectful greeting, my grandparents continued to stare down at me balefully, as if they already knew I would come to no good. I didn't dare stick out my tongue at them, so I saluted, then bowed deeply. I whispered, "Dear Taata's daddy, if you are in heaven, please pray for me. I know we aren't Catholics; I should only pray through Jesus, but all the same, don't let me get punished. I'm just looking at God's beautiful creations, okay? Amen." I felt much better. I always did. My grandfather felt closer to me in heaven than my grandmother in the village.

A huge oval mirror hung in between two columns of chocolate-brown drawers. The mirror turned on its axis, attached to the drawers, and I was always careful not to move it, not to leave any tracks. I dragged a chair up and climbed onto it. The tingliest moment was just before opening the top drawer. Oh, what if there was no brilliance of disorganized rainbow colors as smooth as beach stones, or as rough as sand, and in all shapes possible? But time after suspenseful time, there they were; a confirmation that beauty was magically real. As I slowly opened the drawer, color burst out like flashbulbs popping.

There lay heaps of gold and green, like a strange spicy Asian or Arab dish. The place the jewelry took me to was better than heaven. They were rainbow shells washed up on a fantasy shore. The bead necklaces with matching earrings and bracelets were from Kenya, Nigeria, India, and other countries only traced on maps. The teeny-tiny round colored ants wandered up and down long paths of string in designs of blue and white, or strong red, shiny black, burning yellow; colors of the Uganda flag. There were trembling, see-through, water-blue thick globs of glass. Shiny stones of black and purple that slithered through my fingers like thieves. Pearls of an ivory magnificence that spoke of something deeper than white, something older. Royalty. Angels' tears.

I took it all in as slowly as I could. First with my eyes only, closing them for a moment, then opening them again for the surprise of wild color. Then I passed my hands and arms through the cold stones, slowly turning over the careless heaps, watching them catch the dim light and throw it back in a conversation I understood but couldn't translate. The stones rattled like feisty tambourines, or gurgled low and heavy as they knocked against one another, good luck. I worshiped the color with both hands, rubbing each bead as one would a rosary, then lifted the necklaces up and watched them ripple through my hands like silvery water. My hands warmed them, and then I held them to my cheeks. The smooth stones caressed, the rough beads scratched and tickled. Was this what it was like to be kissed? I breathed in deeply. Ah, Maama's perfume.

That wasn't enough; I had to taste them. I placed one black bead necklace in my mouth and sucked, enjoying its texture and tastelessness. I could hear Maama say, far away in my head, *Get that out of your mouth, you'll fall sick!* That made me suck even harder. What if I swallowed one and choked to death! I would be a princess dying for beauty.

Finally, I put on as many of the necklaces as I could, moving them over my head in worshipful dance movements, head bowed solemnly, then up with secret ritualistic pleasure. My chest grew heavier and heavier as the beads and stones and glass trailed down to my knees. Maama's ears were not pierced, so I could wear her clip-on earrings too. I put on two pairs, feeling them hold on to each earlobe with a sharp, sweet bite. Carefully, I climbed down the chair, necklaces and bracelets and earrings swaying, moved the chair away, and faced the mirror. I leaned forward slowly, sedately, and turned on the lamp covered in red brocade and fringe to match the curtains. I stared at the girl in the orange-reddish glow. Who was she? The rows of glittering color made her beautiful. She could be anyone: a queen, a bishop, a rich loved wife. I passed into blessed existence, where one lived to be beautiful, soft, and rounded out, with red lips, red nails, and glowing stones all over. I was decorated, celebrated, a Christmas tree, here to make the room shine, to turn the world to happiness. I lifted the jewelry and covered my face. I couldn't stay solemn; laughter bubbled up inside. I peeked through the shiny stones and stuck out my tongue. My twin did the same and we giggled. Then I practiced my poses; now a young shy princess, or Cinderella at the ball, up on one foot because of the lost glass slipper. A cardinal waving the sign of the cross through the air, then spraying incense all over. What about a multicolored starfish swirling deep through the azure water of Atlantis? Now, a Paris model posing for flashing cameras, smoking a long cigarette, sending out flying kisses. I could hear the crowd cheer. The jewelry jingled with delighted laughter.

The final act was the best one of all: being my mother. When I grew up, I would use lots of cool white cream like she did: Ponds, Venus de Milo, cocoa butter, perfumes called Lady, Chanel, Essence. I'd paint my fingernails and toenails with designs in glaring red, and fling my hands around dramatically like a conjurer. Wear lots of lacy panties, petticoats, bras, and stockings, all in frilly white and pink, with flowers and sequins, and become Maama. Women were nice and pleasant and sweet, like a bowl of fruit or fresh flowers. Men smelt of cigarettes and beer and wore dull dark colors. The choice was clear.

What would I do then, as a grown-up? I would become real. I definitely wouldn't go back to the village, oh no. An actress on TV, perhaps? I'd have to speak good Luganda, though. Or I'd untie my plaits and pile my long hair up into a glossy crown; it would have grown long, really long, by then. I practiced being a white actress in the mirror, my voice squeaking in a high, fake accent. No, not that; I'd be a president's wife, a good president, not an army man, of course! I'd give money to orphans with beriberi, advise them to eat beans and peas, not just *posho*, which is corn starch and nothing else. In the mirror I ordered my maid, *Bring me some sweets.* Demanded sternly, *Why didn't you wash my panties properly?* I wouldn't go to work, like Maama did; instead, I'd spend the whole day preparing my body, and wait patiently and beautifully for my husband, the president. No, no husband; I'd go to bars every night, like Taata, or to parties!

Maama didn't go out at night, not to parties. Her jewelry was left in the drawers, neglected. Every time Taata went on a trip, he brought Maama beads and pearls as gifts. We didn't mind his traveling; we were freer then, and Maama was ours. And yet, the day he was to come back, the air itself felt different. Maama wore a special dress, usually flimsy, pale pink or blue, and bolder lip-stick. Rusi cleaned out their room thoroughly, and made our supper early so they could eat alone. Sometimes we witnessed the ceremony, the giving out of gifts, if we were quiet and well behaved. Otherwise Taata quickly sent us out of the room. He was like that. He greeted us, me and my older sisters, as a group. "Are you being good at school?" Then we were forgotten. Our new shoes and Christmas dresses were passed to Maama to give to us. He held on to one or two glossy patterned jewelry boxes.

I remember the green stones especially. Taata, an accountant, had come from an international conference in Egypt. The very word, Egypt, spelled magic. I told my school friends every day he was away, "My father's in Egypt," until they got fed up and said, "Stop boasting, you, as if it's you who's there! Why don't you go there and stay!" They were simply jealous, I thought smugly as I flounced away.

Taata brought back maroon tuffets with golden designs of

pharaohs' heads, angular and regal. He brought framed pictures of palm trees and pyramids. But the real Egypt was hidden in the emerald box in my father's hands. I held my breath as he opened it and pulled out, for miles and miles, a dark green snake: grass green, bottle green, lime, first leaves, old leaves, every other shade of green. My breath slowly escaped as the stone trail unwound forever upward like a snake possessed, wooed by my father. Our eyes followed it, worshiping the lacquered stones' dance with the lamplight. Taata walked over to Maama's chair. She was looking at his face, not at the necklace. He placed the box down, held the green rosary in both hands, and said, "For you."

She bowed her head and he gently passed the heavy green stones over her hair and neck, then arranged them carefully on her bosom. We watched as though we didn't know who they were, as though it was a movie. She was crowned; he was her humble subject. She accepted his adoration with a smile in the silence.

We were soon sent off to bed, where I went over the scene, savoring it like an exquisite piece of chocolate slowly melting in my mouth. For you—just like that—for you. He had chosen her. They didn't kiss in front of us, or touch each other, or say dear, unless Taata was drunk. That was embarrassing TV behavior. But who, who would put a string of fire, red, purple, or green, round my neck and say, *For you, Christine?*

I was glad when Taata went on his trips. The house became lighter, and I could shout and run about freely without Maama saying, "Don't disturb Taata, he's watching TV." He's reading, he's sleeping. Don't exist so loudly. We wouldn't have to rush to bed when he came home late in the evening, when he had been drinking, when he became the other Taata, the uglier, noisier one.

Normally, Taata didn't speak to us; he spoke to Maama. If we had something to tell him—school grades, a school trip we needed money for, a telephone message—we told Maama. Sober, he was stern, silent, immobile. How was he moved to buy presents for Maama? What did she do to transform him to warmth, to melt him?

Late at night, when I was already in bed, I sometimes heard the other Taata, the drunk, dancing, rowdy Taata; the one who cried. I rarely saw this opposite of him; that was Maama's private show. He put a blues record on the player and wailed along with it. "My baby's goooone . . ." Could that really be my father? I heard, or did I imagine, the shuffling as he tried to grab Maama and dance. Her muffled protests always ended in silence. I listened, knowing I was far outside their drama. Taata held himself in all day like an ever-present threat, and then at night unleashed himself and his whole tight day on Maama.

As my parents' voices receded toward their bedroom, an argument inevitably began. Taata grunted a word or two, low commas to Maama's continuous sentence of complaint, a wail, a plaintive song. Her voice choked with tears. She seemed to be forcing them back while letting streams of anger pour out. Cowering under my sheets, wide-eyed, I could tell she was trying to keep her voice down, but Taata's short snarls of avoidance made her voice rise and rise like water angrily boiling. "I'm doing everything on my own, everything, while you run around with your friends. Do you know what the children eat, what they wear? Omukikuru, *your own mother*, is sick, but who are your cousins calling? Me! This roof needs repairs; the Rwashibingas need their taps fixed; we have to decide whether to sell that house or not, and what do you do? Drink, drink, drink! I can't do everything, I can't."

Taata woke something up in Maama that drenched her voice with feeling. With us, she was quiet and tired; we worked hard to get her attention. When we told her about school adventures, she simply smiled and nodded absentmindedly. With Taata, Maama was alive—with anger and frustration, yes, but alive. Her voice was rich blood pouring out of a cut vein. Her pain filled my head with all sorts of unnamed feelings, not happiness or sadness but something deeper, sweeter, more horrible. Desire? I wanted to keep on hearing her voice because it was so real. This was who she was, and not just our mother.

We children knew we were an afterthought, outside this world of their own. A heavy door banged shut, sometimes with a sweet word, a gift, but more often with a harsh question, an answering mocking laugh. There they remained; locked in the room of marriage.

Once, I had to get up and use the bathroom near the sitting room because ours wasn't working. I had to. I crept barefoot down the corridor, hoping to slide past the open light of the living room unseen. I did, and saw Taata crying. He was saying,

"Sorry, sorry." I hid behind the long curtains, I just couldn't move away. Maama said, "Stop it, I don't believe you. Stop drinking, or just drink and stop pretending you're sorry."

His heaving pleas rose. "Never again, never, never!"

"Please, Yakobo," my mother whispered to make him stop shouting. "Please, the children are asleep."

"Fuck the children." Loudly, gutturally, as if he wanted us to hear. I did. "Fuck them." So slow he said it, frothing at the mouth, with a drunken swing of his heavy head, as if fuck could not come out easily, as if he had to use each syllable fully to get the meaning out. I didn't know what fuck meant, but the sound of it, the frothy "fff," the relish he added to the "uck" as he said it again, cutting it up, made it dangerous and evil, yet desirable, powerful, eatable, a magical chant against sainthood, guilt, against daylight itself. Ffuuucck. The word hypnotized. It spelled out the need to shock, to be free. To shed daytime silences, restraint, professionalism, pretense. The freedom to drink till he puked. Fuck. As extravagant as the outrageous brilliance of Maama's gold gifts. Fuck as heavy as the green-gold stones. The choking weight of their relationship. A love wrapped in insults and complaints, drunken nights, slobbery sorries, and silent mornings. A strong secret bedroom smell that was very beautiful, and adult, like knowing and using and meaning the word fuck. I was repelled, fascinated, trapped.

After these bitter evenings, the next time I sneaked into their room, I acted out their play as both Maama and Taata. After the first blinding instant of the jewelry drawer opening, I passed my hand through the treasure, sighing. It was safe. Then I put the necklaces over my head, saying, "for you, for you." In front of the mirror I mimicked Maama's high cries, pointing a ringed finger at the mirror. "You bad man, you beer-drinker, you go to dungeons of sin, bring your friends home late at night, and then you refuse to eat your supper. Bad man! We don't see you for days and days. Why don't you take the children for rides or come to Parents' Day at school? If you buy me more necklaces, maybe I'll forgive you. Maybe!"

I turned full circle and faced myself again as Taata, grunting. "I'm so sorry. Beer is sweet and the house is boring. Don't point your finger at me—I'm a man."

Giggling, I fell backwards on their wide rose-covered bed, and the colorful beads and stones jingled. I finally calmed down to silence, let my mind wander through the dim red darkness, and watched the thin arrows of light cut through the curtains. Sparkling dust weaved slowly through the air. I held myself tight and breathed deeply. It was all wound up together, a sweet and painful push and pull, pull and push.

When did they stop talking to each other? Stop trying? When they stopped fighting. When Taata gave up the struggle and got drunk every morning, not just at night. We all got used to it; found it funny even, this dedication to his drinking duties. We had our duties too. They fell on me when my sisters were away. To go pick Taata up from the street when he collapsed on his way home. Answer the door to his fellow drunkards who had lent him money and now wanted it back. Light his cigarettes because he couldn't do it anymore; his hands trembled too much. Wash him when he was ill. He was still our father; we did what we were told.

One day, I came back from school early because I had a cold. I had lost my voice and my nose was blocked, so the P.E. teacher sent me home. I entered the house through the kitchen door. Rusi wasn't there; perhaps she was back in her room I thought. It was very quiet, just like most afternoons. But then I heard murmurs from The Bedroom. No one was supposed to be home. I wasn't afraid, but something made me tiptoe over. The door was ajar, one curtain half open, letting in shafts of light. There was Taata with no shirt on. What was he doing home? I could see he was drunk because his face was an oily brown and he had on a slack silly smile. He was sitting on the bed with no shirt on, no trousers. Rusi was sitting on the floor below him, smiling.

When Taata was drunk he said empty things, talked about himself, about all the great things he had done once, but not anymore, the countries he had traveled to, the awards received, on and on. He needed an audience, but we had got tired of humoring him. That, maybe, was what Rusi was doing, what she was forced to do, to listen to his ramblings. He must have called her into their room, I guess. She had to smile, to pretend to listen to him, to act servile. He had studied in Rome; did she know where that was? He had traveled to Moscow, oh, but what did she know; she had never even seen snow, let alone left Uganda.

How could Rusi refuse to listen? How could she leave? She was the housegirl. She couldn't stand over him; her place was there, on the floor. Rusi couldn't sit on their bed, so she sat on the floor and smiled. She who spoon-fed him when he was weak and delirious after severe drinking bouts. She probably had saved his life more than once. But there she was, not free, like Maama, to unleash anger. Taata still was the boss.

I was stuck at the door, looking at his naked chest, hairless, the light brown color of weak tea. Rusi close by, his knee touching one of her heavy breasts. They both turned to the door; Rusi's smile got stuck in a grotesque grin. Taata raised his arm weakly, slurring, calling, "Patti, I mean . . . Christi . . . is that you . . . Christine, no—you, who are you anyway? Rosa? Come here!" His rising voice woke me up, and for the first time I disobeyed him, ignored him, and walked away. That wasn't my bedroom after all.

My father died fifteen years ago. I moved to the United States, where fuck is an everyday word. I am a woman now, I guess, but so unlike my mother. I don't wear lipstick or makeup or long flowing skirts. I feel silly in them. I don't wear jewelry either. Bright colors look gaudy, cheap, and tasteless in real life. Fake pearls, of course, are fake.

I went home last summer for a visit. My mother is still in the same house. Rusi was sent back to her village after Taata died. Maama said she was missing things, one by one, and who else needed to steal blouses, shoes, but Rusi? I found that hard to believe, after all those years she'd been with us, but didn't say anything. I had never told Maama what I'd seen in their room.

Maama is so much more at ease, and now looks after her grandnieces, children of my cousin who died. She lets them run through the house, even into her bedroom, muddy shoes and all. Is this the same Maama?

One day I found the girls, Nyakato and Kengoma, playing with the magical stones I carried in my mind like recurring dreams.

"Maama! Your jewelry . . ."

She said, "Well, it's old, now."

"Yes but, but—Taata gave it to you!"

"Eeh—Christine, calm down. I never wore it that much, anyway."

I wanted to cry. The glass and stones and beads were much smaller than they used to be. The pearls were a ghastly plastic, peeling even, like children's garish toys. The bead necklaces had hundreds of my lovely little ants missing, the dull bare string hung limp, and the uneven pattern of the remaining beads was like a gap-filled evil grin. My nieces spread them out on the floor and asked me to play with them. Counting games, shooting games, marbles, money games. Not "I am a beautiful princess from under the sea." The secrets the beads shared with me— were they all lies? Who had struck the living stones dumb?

I ran my hands over my favorite, the green and gold necklace from Egypt. It was, surprisingly, still whole. But no longer was it made of the royal stones that charmed King Tutankhamen's daughter, me. No, the stones were the dull, empty shells of dead insects, gray cockroaches, coarse and scratched and old. Faded, the color of dried grass. My nieces didn't mind. "Auntie Christine, those are our coins, worth only one cent each, 'coz they're so ugly."

Maama's room, without Taata, was just like any other. Nice, light, untidy. Where was my father's presence, so guilt-ridden and drunkenly passionate? My grandparents looked old and weak, even though they still stared hard at the camera. Now they looked like they feared the strange instrument rather than disapproved of it.

I blurted out to Maama, "Do you miss Taata?"

She looked at me, mildly incredulous. "What's wrong, Christine?"

"Just asking."

She shrugged and turned to my niece Nyakato, who had come in. What had passed was gone. Why was I searching through ashes? I had lived off his love for her, like a leech. That should have been enough.

ii

Hunger

My PRIVATE Diary
Patti Mugisha
Gayaza High School
Kampala, Uganda, Africa, the Universe

SUNDAY, APRIL 10, 2 P.M.

Boarding school is like purgatory, or prison—being sent away to wait. That's mainly what I do: wait for time to pass. There are five more hours to supper, and I'm hungry already. I'm up here in an empty classroom, writing in my diary when I'm supposed to be studying, 'coz it's one week till finals. Three more long weeks, then home, home at last. Please, God, help me concentrate on this stupid history book. I don't want to study in the dorm with the others. I prefer to be alone with the leftover scribbles on the blackboard and the disorderly desks and chairs abandoned by the last class of girls on Friday. The scratched and beaten-up furniture looks like wreckage after a riot, it's so old.

We had sweet potatoes and peas for lunch: not as bad as the usual mash, but not enough. It's never enough. There is no privacy in the dining room, nowhere to hide. That's what I hate about school. No moment to myself. Even my thoughts feel exposed. We are squashed fifteen girls to a table, girls from all grades, so that we can learn from our "elders." Thank goodness for the wide windows along both sides of the room with their wooden shutters flung open for air and light. At least I can take in the flourishing trees outside.

There is a mural at one end of the room, which I have stared at for three long years now to avoid looking too hungrily at the food being served. I need to disguise my greed. Nobody remembers which art class painted the mural or when. It's one of those paintings that shows every activity under the sun: a church with musical notes sailing out the window to heaven; a school (ours) with classes full of round, dark heads; an airplane flying over cows in a field; a red-orange (but fading) fire in an office building with fire engines and ambulances and running figures around it; a street with small children crossing, holding hands; angels flying in place, stuck in the sky; and the yellow sun above it all. Only the sun isn't shining yellow anymore. All the colors have faded to a grayish-creamish brown that matches the dining room smell of burnt beans, rotting cabbage, oily plastic plates, and about two hundred sweaty girls. I study the busy picture's comic details while wishing and praying for enough food to satisfy my stomach.

Today at lunch it was Joyce's turn to serve my table. As usual, she gave each of us so little I could have cried. After we quickly cleared our plates, there was a long wait while the seniors gabbed on forever about nothing, when they knew very well that the rest of us were waiting for seconds. The dishes are placed at the head of the table where the older girls sit. So even though they are fat enough already, they get second helpings first and finish up all the food, leaving us younger ones staring at our empty, dirty gray dishes that look like shapeless open mouths. Even now, after lunch, my stomach is growling. Oh, God, I pray for something good today instead of all this suffering. You promised to fill our cups to overflowing, told us to "bring your vessels not a few." Amen!

Worst of all is watching Linette not eat because back at the dorm she can slowly munch down a whole packet of biscuits or a loaf of bread. Her father is minister of agriculture; she can afford to play with her dining room food, mashing it into a creamy mess that she stirs round and round her plate. I can't stop staring. Linette brings hot sauce, margarine, or mashed avocado to the dining room—anything to make the weevil-infested beans and *posho* taste like food. Even then, she doesn't eat much of it and makes disgusted faces as we gobble ours down. Oh, I wish I could eat her leftovers. I'd lick the avocado right off her plate. No, no. My Father in heaven fills me. He satisfies my every need. Yes, Lord, I do believe.

I think I'll stay in class. There's no point in going back down to the dorm for tea at four. That sugarless, milkless so-called tea is just bitter black water.

5:30 P.M.

It's so hard to believe in God sometimes, when I think about what He puts me through. And He says He loves me. I went back to the dorm at teatime anyway, because I was so hungry. I trusted God for a miracle. Why not? I am His child, His chosen one. Maybe I could ask Linette to lend me some money, I thought. Just five shillings to buy a few oily *kabs*.

I was going to get my tea when Linette asked me to fetch her some too, because she was busy getting her hair done. She was sitting down between Mary's legs on a sisal mat on the floor, surrounded by the bright black metal frames of our bunk beds. Every week Mary plaits Linette's hair in complicated *biswahili*, and Linette gives Mary grub, hair oil, Cutex, even Colgate.

Mary is basically a *koty*, a servant who works for food, though she would never admit it. Her family never comes to see her; she's from some village deep in Busoga. The teachers give her shoes and clothes and money to get home at the end of the term. You would think Mary would be a nicer person, you know, grateful and humble, but no, she refuses to tie anyone else's hair but Linette's and acts as if her father is a minister too. She even talks fake like Linette and tries to walk like her, throwing her bum this way and that. But Mary has none to throw; she is as flat as a table and tall as a stick, not like Linette, who is short and plump, with the soft, round cheeks of the pampered, as if her mouth is stuffed full of bananas. Together they look ridiculous, although I shouldn't say so, since that's how God made them. I'm sorry, Lord Jesus. Actually, I pity Mary because Linette pretends to be her friend only when she needs her clothes washed and ironed and her shoes polished. Linette's real friends are the posh girls of Sherbonne House; who doesn't know that?

Anyway, as I went to fill my cup, Linette asked, "Patti, fetch me some tea, please?" As if I was her *koty* too.

Then, of all things, Mary reached for her old, stained plastic cup and chimed in, "Me too, Patti?"

"But I've only got two hands!"

They both made faces, then Linette said to Mary consolingly, "We'll share mine; it's okay." She gave me an ugly look, as if I, who was getting her tea, was the mean one.

But I'm a child of God, so, even though I didn't want to, I picked up Linette's cup. It wasn't plastic, of course, but a hard, shiny white decorated with Mickey Mouse figures. Heavy, too, with a handle that burned when the cup was full. But we will be known by our good deeds. Amen.

When I got back with the tea, I decided, in desperation, to shame myself. "Please, Linette, can you give me just one spoon of sugar?"

Mary smugly watched me beg, knowing she was going to get sugar and dried milk and bread and bananas and everything.

Linette didn't even look at me. She just took her cup of tea from my hand and went outside our room to her locker, which is always bursting with grub. She called back, "Mary, *bambi*, my bread has gone stale. Do you mind just having biscuits? Oh, wait, here are some groundnuts."

My stomach growled cruelly, like a dog. "Please, Linette?" My voice squeaked.

She turned around, annoyed, as though I was a dirty fly she couldn't shrug off her shoulder. "Patti, you're always begging. Am I supposed to look after the whole dorm?"

She spoke intentionally loud, right there in the corridor, while girls passed by, going to and from their rooms and lockers. Everybody heard her, and she knew it. My head suddenly clogged up with hate, but I was trapped by my own groveling need. I couldn't look at Linette. Mary's high mocking laughter trilled out of our room. Why didn't I just walk away? I couldn't. More than anything, I wanted the sugar.

"Just a spoon?" I pleaded.

Linette took my cup from me roughly, spilling some of the tea and exclaiming, "Eh! Now look what you have done!"

"Sorry, Linette."

"Don't sorry me. Here's your sugar."

She poured *four* spoons into my cup, not bothering to stop the precious silvery grains from trailing down to the floor. *That* was pure malice. She knew I could have put some of it away for tomorrow, at least. I climbed onto my top bunk and buried my face in my history book. I still feel it. The shame. The frustration. I have no energy for anger.

My tea now was lukewarm and so ghastly sweet it hurt my throat, but I forced it down. I wasn't reading, but thinking, *Oh, God, how unfair You are! How can You give someone this evil all the food and things she has?* Why had I tortured myself by going back to the dorm for tea? I should have stayed in the empty classroom till supper, chewing on my tongue, swallowing saliva.

I wanted to cry. I couldn't ignore those two, who were eating, talking, and laughing as if nothing had happened. Linette usually did all the talking while Mary listened and applauded, acting amazed and impressed by everything Linette said. Being a *koty* wasn't easy. Or did it come naturally to her, the—no, please, God. No bad words. But Mary was the one gobbling down handfuls of groundnuts, not me. Dear God, what sort of lesson am I supposed to learn from this?

I walked back to the classroom, past the dining room and the other dorms, where clusters of girls sat on the verandas, eating all sorts of nice things—*kabs*, roasted maize, biscuits—as they talked and laughed. The cement path up the slope to class was bordered by severely chopped, stifled grass that moved me to pity. It was too neat to be natural, like a newly pressed army uniform.

God says we suffer for a reason. What reason? Maybe, just maybe, God will answer my prayers and Maama will come see me this evening. Or what if Jesus comes back? I mean, *what if?* Oh, the promised Rapture! I would be lifted up with the holy ones, leaving Linette and Mary behind to burn in hell as they screamed and pleaded for mercy. No, that's silly. And evil. Forgive me, Father. Give me a heart to love them no matter what, because right now I don't; I don't love them. All I can think about is my stomach.

I'd better get back to history, which to me sounds like lies: the past reheated as moral tales of good versus bad, strong versus weak. "Shaka Zulu was a man of humble origin," and so on and so forth. It's all about how he fought and killed everybody and became king. All I have to do is quickly cram it in for exams, and then I can just as quickly forget it. But I can't concentrate;

I'm so hungry, so empty. What do I want? I wish a prefect would come running in right now and announce that Maama is here. A miracle! Please, God, please.

7 P.M.

There goes the supper bell, breaking the silence of this long, dreary evening. The clanging means food at least, as bad as it is. And I've finished with Shaka; he's dead. The bell also means the end of visiting hours for the week. That's it. Another five long days of hunger without hope. My Jesus, You alone know what's best for me, but it's getting harder to wait for Your will. It really is.

8 P.M.

We had *cas-kat* for supper: starchy white cassava cooked with fat brown beans. The cassava was hard to chew, but there was a lot of it. Thank you, Jesus! I ate it hungrily. Everyone stared, but what did I care? Shame disappears when hunger arrives. The bell rang before I finished eating, but I wasn't going to leave my food behind. I pretended to ignore the gaggle of girls as they scraped back their benches and streamed out into the cool evening air: carefree and confident, comfortable in the company of their friends. They had nothing to worry about except maybe a few pimples popping up.

Only two other girls remained in the huge, darkened dining room. We silently bent over our plates and our private hungers. It is only the most *maalo* girls who stay behind: the villagers, the greediest ones, the ones who desperately and completely clean their plates of the so-called food. Everyone else stares and snickers at us as they walk out. Us versus them. *Maalo* versus posh. How can we not care what they think of us as we expose our poverty and greed? We are ashamed of having no shame.

The worst of it is, I think I'm better than the villagers. I'm not really *maalo*, not from the village. I grew up in Entebbe. My father used to be a senior accountant with Standard Bank. Taata went to England and Europe many times for work and bought us dresses and shoes you couldn't find in Uganda. I mean, we used to have a Benz! But when his drinking became a day-and-night obsession, he lost his job. It was announced on TV that he'd been retired "in public interest." I don't want to describe that shame.

Now Maama has to dig in the evenings after work and on weekends. She plants beans, maize, *doh-doh*—anything to save money. Poor Maama. She doesn't have a car or the time to come and visit, or the money. Sure, everybody's worse off after Idi Amin's regime, but *we* shouldn't have been. Anyway, why am I writing about this? I'm tired of thinking about these things, chasing what might have been round and round in my head, looking for someone to blame. Why can't I be happy and chatty and simple, like the other girls? Life would be so much easier. Maybe because I am a child of God. He says we are different; we are not of this world. We should not want to be part of it. But I can't help it; I do.

10:30 P.M.

It's after lights out, but I have to stay up and write this. Everything is just like it was before, but different. How can I explain?

After supper, I decided to go up to the chapel for a fellowship meeting. I was tired of pretending to study, tired of the dorm, of the silly talk about nothing, of Linette, Mary, and everyone else. Tired of my own thoughts.

As I walked up the hill through the dark, the chapel glowed weakly in the distance. The cassava sat like a rock in my belly, but still there was an emptiness, and the dull ache of disappointment. Maama had not come. I know she has to do everything herself, and I'm not the only one she has to think about: there are three of us children. God, help Maama, I prayed. Please be good to her. I looked up to the sky, hoping to find . . . what? A sense of God, perhaps, from whence my help would come. Oh, God, please help me, I pleaded. The night answered with a cold silence.

We usually held our meetings in the front part of the chapel, before a large, bare wooden cross hanging high on the whitewashed wall. The only pieces of furniture up in the front are a long, empty table and two benches along each wall. That is the altar: simple, clear, and clean. Down a couple of steps, the rest of the chapel is filled with rows of lean brown benches. For our meetings, we move a few of these into a semicircle. We begin with prayers, then sharing. After three girls' joyous testimonies, I got up.

"Praise God!"

"Praise Him!" the girls chorused back.

"I prayed today for my family to come see me. They didn't. But I am trying to understand that my plans are not the Lord's. His solutions are not my solutions, and I have to be thankful at all times. Even if I am laughed at or mocked or I go hungry or—"

I stopped, confused. What was I saying? I didn't want to talk about the begging incident and shame myself all over again in public. I ended lamely with "Praise God" and crept back to my seat.

The girls murmured with pity, but it didn't feel real to me. What a fool I was. My testimony was pointless and had ended abruptly, unlike the other girls' victorious, God-affirming flourishes. Why couldn't I see the glory of God, instead of concentrating on my stomach? I tell you, hunger is like a child crying and crying: you can't think about anything else.

Intense prayer followed the testimonies. Those already anointed by the Holy Spirit quickly fell into that blessed state; some spoke in tongues. I knelt down, closed my eyes, and waited, tired of pleading. The holy girls' cries rose to a frenzy around me. As usual, I felt separate from everyone else. The light above glowed red through my closed eyelids as I struggled to concentrate on God. Subdued, not anointed, and always hungry: for food, for the Holy Spirit, for a sense of myself as part of this group, my sisters in Christ, or the circle of girls in my dorm, or part of a normal family. To be part of *something*.

For comfort, I started to recite as many promises from the Bible as I could remember: "Do not be afraid; I am with you. . . .

Though I walk through the valley of the shadow of death, I shall fear no evil. Thy rod and staff shall comfort me." But I could not erase the bitter sugar scene from my head. The humiliation, the need gripped me.

One girl's voice rose reedy and high in song:

Even so, Lord Jesus, come
In my heart that I may feel your love.
Though at times I've betrayed your trust,
Even so, Lord Jesus, come.

Everyone joined in, singing and wailing. I remained silent and waited—for what, I don't know. All around me the girls swayed in sweet suffering, relishing the pain of being outcasts on earth, but chosen by God for heaven. Only Jesus could see them through. Only Jesus.

The light seemed to darken behind my eyes. The day's humiliation, hunger, and deep loneliness crept through my body, rising like a dark river, as if to drown me. I was overcome by a strange sadness, as though touched by the sorrow of Jesus Himself. I started to cry and hid my face in my hands, bowing low. I couldn't control myself, didn't want to. The tears came slowly, painfully. I gave up all resistance and let them flow free. Wave after heaving wave washed away my strongly built dam of false hopes and pretensions, my anxious pleas and desperate beliefs. Out flowed the dirt of resentment, bitterness, and blame for my suffering at school. My family's proud history gone horribly wrong. Maama's criticisms, complaints, and endless scraping for money. Taata's hopeless cycles of drinking and trying to stop and failing, then drinking even more in disgust. My family's disgust with him, our shame, our pity. Out poured my own self-absorption and self-pity, which had bound me down, kept me from soaring high into the spiritual, pure and free. All my longings welled up and flooded over. The noisy chapel and its group of greedy saints disappeared as I cried and cried, completely wetting my hands, my face, and the front of my uniform.

After how long, I don't know, I stopped. I was now empty, flat, like a dead fish washed up after a driving storm. Then, a quiet calm crept over me. Sensing silence around me, I opened my eyes and sat down slowly, sniffling a little. The girls next to me fidgeted uncomfortably. I wasn't supposed to cry. I should have spoken in tongues, praised God, and sang, not cried uncontrollably. But that didn't matter. I felt like a newborn baby: simply there.

There were two unsaved girls sitting at the edge of our group. They had come for the Christian show, since there was nothing better to do on a Sunday evening here at this boring boarding school. The two girls stared at me openly, incredulously. Then they began to giggle. I didn't mind. In fact, I wanted to laugh with them. Why not? My mind was a ripple on a calm lake. God had taken me and moved me to some other better place.

At the end of the meeting, we all held hands and said "The Grace." Some girls shot curious glances at me. I couldn't help but smile back. As we walked out, one of the unsaved girls asked loudly, "What's wrong with her? Has she gone crazy?"

Some of the group usually stayed behind after the fellowship, milling and talking and hugging one another outside the chapel. Before today, I would have walked away like a lonely leper, fearing the slightest brush of human contact. But now I stayed, standing at ease in the warm dark air, under the faraway but friendly sky. I could taste peace and it was sweet. I felt warmth for my sisters as they moved through their routine, but I had no need to do so. I felt part of the sky's endlessness and mystery, which flickered down in the long-ago light of the stars, God's messengers. I slowly walked back to the dorm, to all that was waiting, just like it was before.

iii

First Kiss

C hristine's romance was one day old. She was going to meet
Nicholas again this afternoon. It was a hot empty Sunday
in Entebbe, so bright you couldn't see. She didn't want anyone
to know, but wondered how her sisters, Patti and Rosa, could
not sense her excitement. The air itself felt different. Christine
lay in bed late into the morning, plotting her escape. Her first
date! With a boy! She was fourteen. Nicholas was older, eighteen
maybe? Not Nick, or Nicky, but Nicholas. That was classy, she
thought.

Having older sisters made Christine feel and talk older. She
learned a lot that her school friends didn't know, like the words
to more than four Jackson Five songs, and that the fashionable
narrow trousers were called "pipes." Christine couldn't wait for
adult things to happen. To wear a bra for a good reason, dance
at parties, talk to boys nonchalantly, then giggle over them with
her girlfriends. Move to Kampala instead of dying of boredom in

Entebbe. But however much she copied her sisters, she still felt smaller, thinner, inadequate.

Anyway, what would she wear? How would she escape the house without anyone knowing? They would poke their noses into her business, ask her this and that. She had met him, Nicholas, the day before. He was as tall as a windmill. As foreign and familiar as one, too. A boy. No, a man. Help! Christine's world had been made up of women even before Taata died three years ago. He had been quiet and remote or drunk and to be avoided. Her sisters, mother, and aunts had converged protectively over and around her. In primary school it had been a scandal even to *talk* to boys; they were alien creatures.

Nicholas wasn't a stranger, though; she knew the whole Bajombora family. They had all gone to Lake Victoria Primary School—Lake Vic—once the best school in Entebbe. Back before Uganda's independence, in the early sixties, it had been for whites only. Some textbooks still had the stamp "The European School." But by 1973, with Idi Amin's regime in full force, there were about two *bazungu* left in the whole school.

Nicholas's youngest brother had been in her class. Even though the Bajomboras were always last in class, they were the best dressed in the whole school, with sharply ironed khaki shorts, shirts new and dazzling white, and black shoes so shiny you could see your face in them. Not that she got that close; they were boys! Rough and rude, or should have been. Their shoe heels were never worn down to one side like most of the others'; that was a sign of money. The dumb, handsome Bajombora boys, six of them. They were a deep, dark, smooth black and were all prizes. Although they belonged to Christine's ethnic group, the Banyankore, they were Catholics, which made them completely different, at least in her mother's Protestant opinion. To Maama, Catholics were misguided fools, though she never said this, of course, but clearly let it be known by turning down her mouth, raising her eyebrows, and hurrmphing heavily. Don't even bring up Muslims.

The day before, when Christine's sisters were dressing up to go to the Bajomboras' party, she had asked jokingly, "Can I come?" She was bored. She had spent the whole day in bed reading a Georgette Heyer romance. They were best read all the way through, at once, to keep up the excitement. To keep believing, hoping, fantasizing. Fantasy was so much better than real life. Christine became the plucky heroine waving her fan, singing, *"my ship sailed from China / with a cargo of tea . . . ,"* as she strolled through spring gardens or the drafty halls of Rossborough Castle. She inevitably fell in love with the hero, the tall, dark (African?) Lord Wimbledon, long before he won the heart of the rebellious witty heroine, Lady Thomasina. She imagined his shapely thighs in tight white knickerbockers, his ponytail long like a pirate's. No, not a pirate; he was an aristocrat. No one could resist him, not even Lady Thomasina, who had a mind of her own, but no fortune, alas. It was a fun read, but left Christine with a vague feeling of disgust, the same sick satisfaction she felt after eating too many sweet oily *kabs*.

Christine was on holiday, which was better than starving at school, but flat. She listened and watched her sisters talking on the phone, going out, working on their figures, doing sit-ups, drinking endless glasses of lemon juice that supposedly were slimming, walking with books on their heads to learn grace, wrapping their hips tight to stop them from growing too big. Rosa and Patti were seventeen and eighteen. They had purpose. Christine read romance novels and napped.

Rosa brushed away Christine's plea the way she usually did, as though her sister was a bothersome fly. "Don't be silly, the party is not for kids. Me, I won't have time to look after you."

Patti, as expected, took Christine's side. "*Bambi*, you want to come with us? Why not? But ask Maama first."

"Don't waste your time; she won't agree. *Bannange*, who last used the hot comb, and left their *bi-hairs* in it! Eeeh!"

Christine found Maama in the sitting room watching a TV play. *Ensi Bwetyo*—"Life's Like That"—had run forever. Maama was drinking her usual black tea. Christine's voice squeaked nervously. "The Pattis said I could go with them to the Bajombora party."

"Since when, at your age?" Maama talked to the children in Runyankore, but for some reason they answered her back in English. Probably because they would have been punished at school for speaking their own language.

"It's for all ages."

"Are you sure?" Maama's attention was on the TV show; she didn't want to miss a word. Patti came to Christine's rescue. "*Bambi*, let her come. She'll stay with me full-time."

Maama slowly turned her eyes away from the TV and swept her gaze over the two of them, down, up, and back down again, as if she was trying to figure out who they were. She shrugged her shoulders and turned back to the TV, torturing them with time. "Don't come complaining to me about her afterwards," she said. Maama never came right out and said yes. That would be too kind; she might get taken advantage of.

Patti quickly hot-combed Christine's hair in the kitchen while Rosa complained that *the baby* would make them late. The heat of the comb close to Christine's scalp caused delicious shivers of fear down her neck and back. Anticipation felt like a mild fever. She was going to a real party. *Katondest!* she said over and over again silently. Christine's feet were already Patti's size, so she borrowed her sister's pair of red high heels, with long straps that criss-crossed up the calves. She became Lady Thomasina preparing for a ball. She put on a corduroy pantsuit her aunt brought her a year ago from London. It was getting too small; it pressed into her crotch and squeezed into the crack of her bum, but what else could she wear? At least it was the latest, sort of. She almost twisted her back trying to see her behind in the mirror. Rosa laughed. "No one's going to notice *you*, silly!"

Patti came to Christine's defense, "*Wamma* you look good, grown-up."

Rosa jeered back, "*Kyoka*, Patti, you can lie!"

"How come the Senior Fours borrowed it for two socials last term? It's still in." Christine posed dramatically in front of the mirror, one hand on her nonexistent hips.

"Lie yourself, then! It's not the trousers that are the problem; it's your stick figure. Anyway, let's go!"

Christine and Patti were used to Rosa's taunts; they simply ignored her. Patti drew dark eyebrows over Christine's own and painted her lips deep crimson. Christine was startled by her reflection, and Rosa laughed hysterically. "Don't let Maama see you!"

"No one will know she's fourteen." Patti was proud of her artwork.

Forget her face; Christine's worry was falling off the high heels, since they were walking to the party. It had just turned dark when they set off. The air was bluish, mysterious, and the crickets shrilled urgently, but the girls did not hear them. Each of them dwelt on her own separate excitement. Rosa was going to see Sam, her boyfriend, again. She preferred being with him in public, showing off their love, rather than when they were alone, which time she spent fighting off his roaming hands. That wasn't romantic. As for Patti, she was saved, but didn't believe dancing was a sin. She danced for the Lord, she said, like David in the Psalms. Okay, David hadn't danced "squeeze" with women, but neither did Patti with boys. Nor did she drink. Patti was a little worried about Christine, however, who was more like Rosa, in Patti's opinion, or at least wanted to be, which could be worse.

Christine almost fell a number of times in the high red shoes. The tarmac road, which had not been repaired since the late sixties, before Amin took over, was more like a dry riverbed. Most of the tarmac was gone, leaving huge potholes to be skirted around. Luckily it hadn't rained recently, so there were no pools of muddy water, only empty craters and dusty flyaway soil and stones. Cars that circled off the road to avoid the potholes had widened it, creating yawning mouths with no teeth, only gaping dirty-brown holes. It was safer to walk down the middle to avoid the cars that bumped and swerved along the roadside. It would have been better with no tarmac at all. The girls walked with heads bowed down out of habit, picking their way through unthinkingly. They did not see the solemn indigo beauty of the sky, now glowing with far-off dots of light.

When they got to the party, Christine hung close to Patti shyly until she saw Betty, the Bajomboras' cousin, who lived with them. She was two years older than Christine but had repeated classes in primary school, and so had ended up in P.7 with Christine. Betty already had full breasts by then, when everyone else had nothing or only tiny protruding plums that stretched their school uniforms tight across the chest. One year later, at fourteen, Betty got pregnant and had an abortion. It was a major scandal. She was sent to her village, Ibanda, for a year. She came back subdued, fat, and very *shera*, you could tell her tribe right away. She said *mwana* all the time, and walked as slowly and as heavily as a cow. Well, that was considered graceful among the village Banyankore. Christine had seen Betty only twice since that time, by accident, but was so glad to see her now, especially since she didn't want to trail after Patti like a five-year-old. Betty looked like a woman, but, thank goodness, she didn't brush her off.

Betty gave Christine whisky mixed with Mirinda to cut the sour taste and hide the alcohol. Christine didn't say she had never drunk whisky before. She was surprised by how it burnt going down, not like pepper, but like glowing warm fire. The two girls danced together; they could do that, they were young enough. But then some strange boy called Betty outside, pointing with his head, and off she went. Too willingly, Christine thought. She was alone again. She was supposed to be having fun with other people; that's what parties were for. Luckily or un-luckily, Patti saw Christine and asked one of the Bajombora boys, Nicholas, to dance with her. He looked drunk, and smiled at Christine like he was doing her a favor. It was a Congolese song, and it seemed to last forever. The dance was simple, dull, and repetitive: one step left, then back, another right and back, left, right, with an accompanying jiggle of the hips. Nicholas danced in his own stiff way, frowning with concentration. It made her smile. He noticed and smiled back, then said, "You're a good dancer," leaning over her as if he was about to topple. He was tall, tall. The Leaning Tower of Nicholas. She smiled at her own joke and stumbled on his foot. "Enough," he laughed. "Let's have a drink."

"Not in front of my sisters."

"Outside, then."

They sat on a low branch of a huge old mango tree. It wasn't mango season, but the leaves were heavy and reassuring, a dark green umbrella for everyone, a rich auntie. Christine wondered where all the ants that crawled the craggy bark of every mango tree went to at night. Nicholas had put more whisky than Mirinda into Christine's drink. It burned her throat and brought tears to her eyes. She forced it down with a cough. Then it seemed like a bright light turned itself on in her head as they sat in the warm clear dark. The stars, which she usually didn't notice, twinkled in an exaggerated way through her tears. Christine stopped herself from showing him the sky; that would be silly, but she bet Lady

Thomasina would have. What next? Nicholas lit a cigarette and inhaled deeply. He didn't say anything. But somehow, casually, his arm went over her shoulder. He put out his cigarette on the branch, then his face closed in and his lips were on hers. "My lipstick!" she thought, as he chewed away at her lips, then snaked his tongue into her mouth and ate some more. His smoky smell reminded her of her father. Soon, she couldn't breathe, didn't know how to, but just in time, he broke away. "Nice," he said, as she wiped her mouth with the back of her hand. She jumped off the branch. "Wait, don't go," he said.

"Patti will be looking for me."

"Okay, why not meet me tomorrow? Christine?"

She cleared her throat. The whisky, or something, was bubbling in her brain.

"Where?"

"How about at Lake Vic? The school, not the hotel. In front of the Assembly Hall, okay? Around two?"

"Okay."

So *that* was kissing. That was it? She couldn't decide if it was yucky or nice. She wiped her lips with the back of her hand. Would Lady Thomasina be this confused? Would Rosa? Christine had been kissed before Patti, she was sure. Her head felt foggy. Was it the whisky, Nicholas, or both? What if Maama smelt her breath? But *he* wanted to see her again. To kiss her some more!

So there was Christine the next morning daydreaming in bed, and panicking too. It was already eleven, but staying in bed was about the only way to be alone in the shared room. What would she wear? Should she put on lipstick again? Nicholas must have liked the red. Her lips' natural color was a pinkish brown, which just wouldn't do. And what if she looked completely different without her eyebrows drawn over? Should she wear her blue jean skirt, or the yellow lace dress? No, it was too frilly; she'd look like a baby. But she couldn't borrow clothes from Rosa or Patti without being asked a million questions. Imagine, *she* had a date, and with an older man! Well, okay, a boy, but still a date. Look at her fingernails, bitten short and ugly. Had he noticed them yesterday? She hoped not.

One could never tell what was going to happen. The future, the not-yet. It was like reading a book. But with a book, the delicious end was right there in your hands; all you had to do was read and not peek ahead, and you'd get to it. Of course, with romance novels you already knew that the Lord would get the Lady, or was it vice versa? How, was the question, the thrill. In real life, the future didn't exist. You could try and make it up as you went along, like how you put on makeup deliberately, but when other people were involved, there was no way you could tell what they would do. You couldn't control them. They might turn away, or prefer sad endings.

Luckily for Christine, Maama had gone to the neighbors; Mrs. Mukasa was sewing her a dress. Patti had been sent to line up for sugar. Rumor was that one store in Kitoro had some; the owner's son was in the army. Rosa had refused to go. She spent her afternoons "borrowing books," which they all knew meant seeing Sam. That day, Christine was supposed to clean the living room, which she did quickly. She ate leftover cassava and beans for lunch, enjoying the rarely still, empty house, then bathed and dressed up, slowly, deliberately. She chose the blue jean skirt; it was casual but looked good. She wore a red top to match Patti's red shoes, which she borrowed again for good luck. There. Christine went out through the back door to the boys' quarters, where Akiki, the housegirl, was resting. Christine called out through her closed door. "Akiki, the house is empty. I'm off to Betty's," and rushed away before Akiki could get up and see her all dressed up.

Christine slowed down once she got to the street. She was sweating already. Why did Nicholas choose the afternoon? It would have been cooler later on, and the evening light more romantic. Christine giggled and practiced a womanly sway. The high heels definitely made her more feminine, though unbalanced. She smoothed her jean skirt over her still small hips. Was it the heat or this escapade that was making her leak sweat like a broken tap? Under a jacaranda tree by the side of the road, she got a small mirror, Patti's, from her bag, rubbed on Patti's lipstick, then walked on.

Everything was asleep; the road was dead, even the flies were too lazy and drunk with heat to do more than flop around. The sun was Christine's relentless witness. She reached the huge roundabout in front of Lake Vic, but had to walk around it because the grass was overgrown. Back when she and her school friends passed by every day on their way to school, they would find groups of five or six women hired by the Entebbe Town Council cutting the grass with long thin slashers. The women were always busy because the grass grew back as fast as ever. Poor women; during Amin's "economic war" they were paid next to nothing. It now looked like the council had long given up the fight with nature. The grass, ignoring the emergency situation, kept on growing.

Christine could almost see those early morning scenes: most of the slasher women had babies tied onto their backs, who slept peacefully even as the women swung up and down, up and down with labor. The women wore old, faded *busutis* and head scarves wrapped shabbily over their hair. They were barefoot or wore thin rubber *sapatu*. They didn't speak English, of course. Christine and her friends didn't greet them, even though they looked just like their aunties back in the village, whose close, sticky hugs smelt of sweat and kitchen-fire smoke. They were comforting and discomforting all at the same time. But here in town, the lesson these women gave was so clear no one even said it: Study hard, speak English well, get into one of the few good high schools, go to college. Onward and upward. You are not these women. Do not become them.

It was now half past one. Christine was rarely early for anything, but this time she was almost at the school. Past the roundabout was a giant tree that seemed to have retained its immensity even as the school buildings ahead shrank as she grew older. It was an olive tree, though she didn't know that when she was at Lake Vic. The fruit, *empafu*, were green, hard, and bitter, or black, a little softer, but just as bitter. Christine grew to like their chewy texture; it was like an interesting thought to be turned over and over. The fruit left her tongue and inner cheeks rough, as though her mouth had become someone else's. That was the taste and feel of walking home from school all those years ago. The sound of the past was of the small hard fruit falling. They would drop on her head, plop! or just miss her, startling her out of her daydreams of being first in class; of how she would show them, whoever they were, after whatever slight; dreams of visiting an aunt in Kampala; of going somewhere even farther away, England perhaps. America! As her mind roved, she climbed on the curb, carefully balancing, her arms stretched out wide like wings, one foot straight in front of the other. She was a ballerina, a flying airplane, then plop! The hard nut's sudden fall surprised her into tripping. On other days, when she walked home with her friends Carol and Karen, they would playfully push each other off the black and white curb. Christine could almost hear the laughter, the running, the joking shouts of abuse. All those days merged into one carefree moment in her mind.

Now, the curb's paint had faded to gray and its edges crumbled to dust. All the same, Christine stepped up onto it, stifling a giggle. In Patti's red high heels, she felt like a chicken clumsily trying to fly. Her laughter rang out in the silent hot afternoon, making her catch herself. Nicholas would think she was crazy!

Here was the Upper School Assembly, another faded apology of its former imposing blue and white state. It was now ten to two. Christine was early, oh no, a sign of desperation. Coming on time was bad enough. This was a date, not a school appointment. She wished she had asked Patti or Rosa for advice. No, not Patti, she didn't go out with boys; she would have stopped her from going, called up the Bajomboras or something! Rosa wouldn't be much help either; she would have laughed at her and kept bringing it up forever to embarrass her. So much for big sisters. Well, she had the time to cool down, wipe off the sweat, check her lipstick.

Christine sat in the shade on the cement ledge in front of the Assembly Hall. She doubted the toilets were open or clean. She wouldn't look at her watch again. The Assembly had long glass doors all along one side to keep it cool, and long windows on the other. Some of the panes were cracked or empty. She looked into the darkness of the hall. As her eyes adjusted to the dark, the forms inside took on recognizable shape. What a mess. The curtain on the stage was torn; a piano's dark bulk squatted awkwardly to one side on only two feet, its lid broken and askew. A few small chairs were scattered around the huge dusty floor, and on one of them was a pile of neglected, ragged-looking exercise books. It was hard to believe this was the same school that had performed so well once that even Amin's children had joined it for two terms when they lived in Entebbe State House. It was only three years since Christine had left P.7; how come she hadn't noticed this mess? This *we-have-given-up-why-bother* state. Things must have started falling apart years ago. She hadn't noticed it then, probably because she was here every day. The change was gradual and the result normal, like many other things about Amin's time, including the everyday fear in the air. She remembered how everyone had laughed in astonishment, then got used to it, when Amin by decree banned minis and wigs. He made Friday, the Muslim day of prayer, a day off and Saturday a workday. Everyone adjusted to the upside-down week, the upside-down life, including other unbelievable and ugly things she didn't want to think about. The bad smell became familiar.

In this very hall, Christine had been through five years of morning hymns, prayers, and announcements. She remembered the cheerful routine of singing "We Wish You Many Happy Returns of the Day" for different students every week. The word "returns" had puzzled her; it still did. The headmaster, fat round Mr. Mubozi, had led assembly since Christine's first year in the Upper School, when she was eight. He looked kind and jolly, like Father Christmas, but he wasn't, oh no! She remembered him shouting at a kid once, "Wipe that grin off your face!" Everyone looked around in astonishment for a green face. Christine had gone to his wife's nursery school. She was white. She too was fat and round, but kind, giving them homemade toffee every week. The nursery school was a room at her house, with children's colorful drawings up on every wall. Most of the other kids were Indian. The lasting impression of that year was of their heavy black hair and spicy smell, and how they jostled up to the front, not afraid to seek the teacher's attention, while Christine hung back, waiting, as she had been taught to do. But in one week that year, 1972, the Indian kids disappeared; Idi Amin sent them all away. Christine remembered busloads of frightened faces heading down Circular Road past Saint John's Church to the International Airport, and the piles of comics and all sorts of toys she, Rosa, Patti, and so many others got for almost nothing. Those Indians were rich! Where were all those kids now? Christine wondered.

It was now ten past two. *Okay, calm down,* Christine told herself. At least she was in the shade. Out in the sun, two yellow butterflies chased each other round and round. At the corner of the school building was a huge flower bed with three plants. Someone had planted only three of them. Strange, this neat flower bed next to the dilapidated hall. God, it was quiet. Well, private too, which was good. How come there was a cooling wind in the shade and none in the sun? she wondered distractedly. She should have brought a book. She remembered the dirty book she had seen peeking out of Rosa's suitcase, about a year ago. There was a naked woman on the cover, her body twisted in a weird position. Christine's face went hot as she peeked through the pages. How could Rosa read this? People didn't really do these things! But Maama and Taata must have, at least three times! Christine now giggled at the thought, then guiltily murmured, Taata, rest in peace.

Goodness, two-thirty. Should she leave? Christine heard a clamor of voices and froze. A group of rough-looking kids came running by, boys chasing girls, dark round heads bobbing, all of them screeching and yelling as they ran past, wove round the corner, and, just as suddenly, went out of sight. Silence rose up and took over again. What was she doing there? Christine decided to walk around the school once. Nicholas would have to wait. She would not think past that.

Christine peeked into the P.3 classroom. The chairs were so tiny. Innocent looking. This was where her class had done experiments with beans, to see what made plants grow. They tried to grow one plant without light, one without water, one without soil, and one that got everything. It was science in a bean shell. A guided experiment about life that you could control and be sure of the results. How simple. A few years later in P.7, as a prefect, Christine had stood sternly like a policeman in this very class, tapping the end of a stick on one of her palms slowly, threateningly, barking *silence!* at the smaller kids. It had been a serious game.

Here was the P.4 classroom, where one of the Bajombora boys, not Nicholas, had jumped through a window because of a fire. It wasn't a real fire; someone had shouted *Fire!* as a joke, and he got scared. He jumped and broke his leg and became a mini-hero, even though the whole incident was laughed at. Girls didn't talk to boys, oh no, but they gossiped about boys all the time. How stupid he was, they said, as they secretly admired him. Christine would never have dreamt she'd be here waiting for his big brother.

Christine came to the steps where she had fought with Karen and Carol, her two best friends. It was a game at first: the person in between the other two was the queen. They playfully pushed at one another to get into the center, but gradually the game turned from playful to rough to mean. Before long Christine, the smallest, was pushed to the ground crying, while the other two ran home separately. She was left there sniffling, wiping off the mud. The next day they pretended nothing had happened, but were shame-faced and awkward with one another. They didn't speak about it ever, but now they knew that friendship was envy, admiration, anger, and longing all mixed together. Three years later, Carol's parents retired and the family moved to their village in Toro. Karen went to a different high school. The flow of letters between them gradually dried up. Had all that emotion been for nothing after all? Time passed by and stole it away.

And now, now, time was moving too slowly. Christine circled back to the huge silent Assembly. No Nicholas. A part of her couldn't believe it. So he actually wasn't going to show up. Had he even planned to? Anyhow, had she really, really expected *him* to come and see *her*? That would have been the shock. She should leave. But she wanted to sit there and wait. Just sit there. Not go on. Tear out the end of this book.

Christine's feet in borrowed grown-up shoes hurt her. She undid the long red straps. She was tired of this place, the whole of Entebbe, in fact, filled with buildings that had been alive in the past, but now were small and irrelevant, ruins, almost. The three flowering plants, the only sign of new life around, now looked so stridently and annoyingly red and perky. She glanced over her shoulder then went and pulled at the plants roughly. The stems were tougher than she was; taut, elastic. She tore at the tender petals. The flyaway pollen made her sneeze. She used her hand to wipe her nose and cleaned it off on her skirt, staining her nice tight jean skirt. That made her even angrier. Christine pulled harder at the green stems, leaning her body back. *Aaaah*, she felt the roots tearing, the dark brown earth moving, loosening, the plant breaking free. The release made her stumble back, almost fall, and she laughed through her tears, holding the limp, useless plant in her hands. Now there was soil all over her borrowed open-toed shoes and her feet. She threw the plant carcass back onto the soil, disgusted and feeling silly. Childish. Christine wiped her tears with the back of her hand and cleaned it on her blouse, smudging it red and brown with lipstick, tears, and dirt. What a mess. Nicholas should see her now. She had better go home; they would all be back, asking for her. Maybe there would still be some cookies left for tea.

iv

Passion

You know how we're taught to throw superstition aside and move forward into the modern world? Or maybe you don't, but for us here at Gayaza it's a recurrent theme. Gayaza High School, Kampala, Uganda, for your information. The world's center of boredom. We are forced to find ways to entertain ourselves; it's no wonder a rather fantastic *juju* experiment conjured its way into my head and took over. I was irritated by all the propaganda against "black magic," and the way it was insistently pounded into our supposedly still-soft heads. I mean, why insist so strongly against *juju* if it doesn't exist? If it really has no power? I know, I know, Livingstone or someone said something declaratory against disease, superstition, and backwardness in Africa. I've heard it one too many times.

Anyway, I decided, after listening to yet another Sunday sermon on the topic (yes, we get lectured on it both in class and in church), that I simply would not accept this. As if I had a choice. Let's just say I did have a choice. I would, at least, first find out for myself whether *juju* worked or not. Logical, no? So this is my story about an exploration into our darkest heritage. The womb of knowledge perhaps. Ready?

I should start with who, what, and where. Okay, my name is Rosa. I am seventeen years old and in Senior Five, that's H.S.C.— High School Certificate—or A-levels, at Gayaza, a girls' boarding school that used to be a missionary school way back in the colonial days. You would think it is still one now, what with all the "savedees," i.e., born-again Christians, running around, and the old white British women who won't relinquish power because they can no longer go back home after more than forty years here. What would they do there, poor women? One winter would kill them, and they wouldn't have anyone to lord it over except aides in nursing homes. You should see the *bazungu* here, so know-it-all and steely-gracious before wide-eyed, frightened, and secretly-glowering-with-anger "natives," namely us. Really, this is *not* meant to be a tirade against the hardy old ladies, who faced army men with guns for our sakes during the Amin days and each coup thereafter, and are still alive to tell the harrowing tales. Their *juju* must be stronger, ha ha.

A little bit of gossip may be necessary at this point. Miss Straw, the headmistress, is said to have lost her betrothed in the Second World War, when she was just eighteen. This explains her vacant blue stare: it is the faraway dreamlike look of lost romance; her eyes as blue as the vast ocean her young soldier drowned in. No one knows who started this rumor; it's so old it has become true. In a minute, though, she can turn those eyes on you with chilly hostility and hiss like a plump white snake: "This just will not do!" No lover would have dared woo her then, let alone a trembling student appeal for mercy.

Okay, on with the story. I just wanted to show you what we are dealing with here. So, in Higher, as it's called, we have this extra duty in school and as privileged young women in Uganda, a third world country, don't you forget, because we are getting this excellent, government-subsidized (white) education. We must represent all the impoverished throngs who are not as lucky as we are, especially the women. We must be graceful, hardworking, and upright; disciplined enough to withstand the hordes of lusty men at university, in offices, or on the street who will try to "spoil" us—unless, of course, they want to marry us. Then, as educated, faithful wives, we will work alongside our Christian husbands in our modern civilized homes (bedsheets folded to make perfect hospital corners), while serving our country in a lauded profession. I won't forget Miss Straw at our first assembly in Higher saying, "You must not disgrace Gayaza, this great school that very few have the privilege of joining. The *"privilege,"* she repeated sternly, as if saying *"punishment,"* as she slowly swept her glassy blue eyes over our sea of black heads. Like she was the queen or something!

So now in Higher our uniform is a skirt and blouse, not those O-level dresses that billow out like parachutes unless held down by belts. Cotton belts that have to be starched hard every week simply as a form of torture. And their colors! The brightest, most frightful blue, green, purple, and yellow. You would not believe that the Kiganda "traditional" dress was designed at Gayaza; that's why it's called a *bodingi*, for boarding school, or *gomesi*, after an enterprising Goan tailor named Gomez. So much for tradition. But where was I? Oh yes, we Highers are now considered adults; we have to show the younger girls how to lead Uganda into its (we hope) glorious future. We do this by walking with *digi*—dignity—slowly swaying from side to side, now that we have breasts and hips to carry, as well as huge black files full of notepaper that show we are clearly above and beyond the exercise books the Senior Ones to Senior Fours use.

Another of Miss Straw's feature lectures is that the "A" in "A-levels" does not stand for apathy. That's her attempt at a joke. She even once slouched across the front of the assembly, showing us how our slow sway was a sign of lack of purpose in life. How we laughed that day. "Shoulders back! Behind and stomach in! Walk like you mean it!" Someone should have told her to stick *her* nonexistent butt out.

Enough of that. Here comes the juicy part. Have you heard the myth about safety pins and men? I didn't think so. Let's see, who first told me about it? It must have been Nassuna. We have shared dorm rooms since Senior One, so we've been through everything together. She's Muslim, but doesn't use her Muslim name, Halima; she prefers her Kiganda name. There we were, back in Senior Three, I believe, in Kennedy House, donated by the "People of the United States of America," as was written on a little plaque stuck to one of the walls of the laundry room.

It was after lights out, which is the best time to gossip. Sometimes the teacher on night duty would come around with a torch and quickly open the door to try and catch us talking or giggling in bed. In the dark you couldn't see who it was, all you saw was a glimmer of torch light, unless it was one of the *bazungus*, Miss Hornbake or Miss Simpson (Miss Straw wouldn't lower herself to stalking). In that case you saw a ghostly pale face, wrinkles and white hair gleaming, and that would shut you up with fright pretty fast. Whoever it was would threaten us with being entered into the Red Book, which usually meant standing under the Punishment Tree right in front of the staff room. It sounds like a joke, but imagine the cutting words of all the teachers coming in and out of the staff room, while you stood there exposed, looking foolish. As if you had asked their opinion. Of course, you were not allowed to sit down; it was a punishment, not an afternoon off. As the sun blazed away (it always did), two or three classes would pass by on their way to the labs or the sports fields for P.E. That meant about sixty girls gawked and giggled at you as they ambled past, as if they had never seen anyone stand under a tree before. Ask me if I had been there. I preferred the afternoons at the farm digging or clearing up pig poo, however much more I sweated and stank.

My point is that it was important not to get caught as we learned about *real life* from our roommates. In the dark, in bed, we stuffed our mouths with sheet and blanket to hide our laughter or gasps of fright, but as soon as the teacher left, we continued on in excited whispers. As voices and giggles streamed through the dark, we listened to stories about ghosts and powerful *juju*, and learned what's what about sex, imagining all the gory details. How men were strange, illogical in their cravings; so this was what you had to do to get them. Never answer back, and have no less than three boyfriends: one for love, another for money, and the third to marry. But what was best: looks, money, or brains? These debates raged on night after night; they never lost their intensity and flavor. How many abortions did you say Miss Konkome had before she got saved? Noooo! It's true, I swear. Konny, the one who acts like she's been in deep prayer since she was born? Ah-haaa! People get saved out of *despa*—desperation—nothing else!

My good friend Nassuna always had something to say. She's the one who brought up the story of men and safety pins, claiming that they made men "react." We all went, "What?" "How?" "What do you mean, react?"

"Well, you know, get excited."

"Excited?"

"*Bannange*, do you want me to—okay, they expand, swell . . . you know."

We shrieked, then remembering it was lights out, whispered, "Ee-eeh, Nassuna, *naawe*! Stop lying. Safety pins?"

"Yes, I swear to God." She licked her pointing finger, slashed it across her throat, then pointed up to heaven. God slice her dead if she was lying! "This girl, Namata, remember her? She finished S.4 last year. We both did housework in the classrooms together; that's when she told me. She said men have this problem of wanting women too much, and they can't control it, so we have this power over them."

"What power?"

"Well, it's easy, actually," she whispered confidently, as if she had done it. "You secretly, *secretly*, mind you, rub a safety pin while looking *directly* at the man you like, and you'll get him excited. Just like that. Then he will do anything for you."

"*Kyoka*, Nassuna! Men aren't that weak or stupid!"

"I'm telling you."

Another girl said, "Okay, they do what you want, but they also want something, am I wrong?"

We all squealed and shouted, "Whaaaat?" "Something?"

"But of course!"

We laughed in shock and exhilaration. Oh my God, sex! That unmentionable, dirty, shameful, and most fascinating thing. Something men wanted from us that we could give out, or not, at will. Something to bargain with. Imagine that. Slowly, eventually, we calmed down. It was late, almost eleven. We had to get up at 6:30 for housework or P.E. before breakfast and class. Most of the girls might have forgotten this juicy bit of talk, but I hadn't. I stored it away, even as I thought, what rubbish!

Well, three years later the idea popped into my head one day during English Lit. class. Guess who was teaching? The one and only Mr. Mukwaya, the Walking Wodo. He is the hero of this tale, actually. The other hero, I mean. For those of you lucky enough not to have come to Gayaza, Wodo is short for "wardrobe," which is what Mr. Mukwaya looks like. He is tall, straight, stiff, and thick. Our teachers are picked out at circuses or museums, I swear. I could describe them all and you'd think I'm adding *supu*, soup, but I'm not exaggerating, they really are God's experiments at unique human shapes. God says, "I am bored. Let me make a ball of a woman," and Miss Okello appears, as short as she is wide, fat, and dark, dark black, shiny black, a black so deep you dream of disappearing into it. You can't, though; she doesn't keep still long enough. She runs everywhere. If you see her far off down the path, you may think a huge wheel has escaped off a car and is careening on its own wild way. Despite all her weight, she is so fast. Okello, *duka*! Okello, run! girls call out and duck as she swivels around to chase after the mischief maker, shooting pieces of chalk like bullets. As she runs, she throws sharp words at anyone on her path. All this, surprisingly, makes her a thrilling history teacher. Once you get used to the rapid tat-tat-tat as she spills out words, sentences, ideas, dates, you enjoy how she spins tales out of the past while moving roly-poly round the room. Your eyes and mind blink and move just as rapidly to keep up with her. It's exhilarating. Exhausting, too, by the end.

Oh, sorry, sidetracked again. She's just one example, though. Another that's more to the point is Walking Wodo. He teaches literature, which I love. Well, some of the books. No teacher can spoil novels for me; I soak them up like blotting paper. I wish I could say the same about plays and poetry. Don't make me read poems so clever and chock-full of words they mean nothing. I can make up something to say in class, though. Literature papers? Easy. Just write something about character and theme, whatever the teacher wants to hear. Mr. Mukwaya shares my delight in stories, but he is more extreme. He completely forgets about us, forgets *himself*. You should see him; he enters a trance. He gazes out the window as if inspired by heaven itself, or turns to the blackboard, his back to us, and traces over what he has already written, looking like a huge insect trying to crawl up the board.

It's not Wodo's fault, though, that we're assigned books that bore most of us to tears. For example, we have to do one Shakespeare play for the A-level national exams. Ours is *King Lear*. But who wants to read about the travails of a stupid old man who gives everything away? Serves him right, I say. And why in this ancient, unclear so-called English? You wouldn't believe it, but the language sends Wodo into raptures, especially when Lear is running around naked in the rain abusing his daughters! *"Blow, wind, crack your cheeks! . . . Rumble thy belly full, spit fire, spout rain . . ."* Wodo quotes whole passages and then starts arguing, first with us, then with himself, getting more agitated by the minute. Could King Lear have acted any other way? Wodo asks. Was Lear "more sinned against than sinning"? We turn to one another, roll our eyes, and sigh heavily.

That was the scenario the day the safety pin idea came back to me. I was wondering whether anything at all could distract Wodo from his *King Lear* fantasy and bring him back to this world, right here to us. Did he have a personal life apart from books? This would be a perfect way to find out! And remember, I wanted proof for or against the power of *juju*. I giggled to myself at the thought of the experiment. It was ridiculous, so much so that it refused to leave my mind. I spent the rest of that class plotting ways and means.

Later that evening, Nassuna and Mary and I met for our study group. This is another good thing with Higher, we don't have to go up to class for prep time anymore; we can stay in the dorms and fool around or study, as we wish. We are supposedly mature enough to use our time properly. The pressure of preparing for national exams to enter the only university in the country is supposed to force us to be serious. It works for most of us. I confess I'm lazy, so I rely on study groups, where I can milk others while enjoying the *kaboozi*, good sweet talk, which is my specialty.

That evening I made *bushera* for the three of us. One of the advantages of coming from western Uganda is that we have a lot of millet, which we eat or make into a porridge called *bushera*, or *bush*, as we Gayaza girls call it. It is so filling, which always helps at school, what with *starvé* and all. All you do is add boiling water, but you've got to stir the mixture frantically or it will "die." Thank goodness, in H.S.C. *starvé* doesn't hit us so badly because we are allowed to go home one weekend a month and bring back more supplies of sugar, groundnuts, *mberenge*, and any other grub that wouldn't go bad. The suffering of O-levels was in the past, for the most part. I know, I keep getting sidetracked, but I'm trying to give you the whole picture, okay?

Anyway, there we were talking, our books neglected on our laps. We had heard that Jolly, one of our classmates, had gone to Makerere University to see some guy instead of going home for her day off. To make things worse, she had stayed one night! The only way you could do that was if your parents, and *only* your parents, asked for permission in advance, in writing, or had really good reasons like a death or something. And your parents, not anybody else, had to bring you back to school. It was serious.

Mary asked, "How could Jolly do something so stupid? Now she'll get expelled."

Nassuna answered in her usual know-it-all way, "*Munnange*, it's love. It makes you do crazy things. Her campus boy must have convinced her."

Mary, ever the strong-willed iron woman, scoffed. "*I* wouldn't do it just because some *campus boy* asked me to. Destroying my future just like that. I mean, what is she going to do now?"

"Finish her A-levels somewhere else, Kampala S.S.S., or someplace like that."

"And fail."

"Eee-hh, Mary, are you saying all those in city day schools fail? In fact, they probably have an advantage since their teachers cheat and get them the exams early."

We laughed. "Nassuna, stop lying," I said. "No, I think the real problem is we girls are weak. Anything a man says, we obey."

"Aaa-ahh, not me!"

"Not you, of course, Mary, you have never done anything you don't want to do, right?"

"Not with a boy; she hasn't had the chance."

We laughed as Mary made a mock-angry face and turned away. I went on, "Listen, women have power over men, too. Remember, Nassuna, what you told us, was it in S.2 or S.3, about a trick some girl told you that makes men weak."

"What?"

"Don't you remember? The safety pin thing?"

"*Kyoka*, Rosa! Did you really believe that? And you stored that all these years?"

"Her head is empty, there's space for such!"

I waved down their laughter. "No, seriously, think about it. We have physical power over men 'coz of sex, even though they are supposed to be stronger than us, physically."

"Ya, sure, if you believe in witchcraft!" More laughter.

"You laugh now, but wait till I try it."

"What?" Nassuna and Mary together.

"You heard. I'm going to test to see if it works or not. We're here at school to *study* and *observe* and draw conclusions, right?"

"And there'll be an exam afterwards, I suppose?" That was Mary, Miss Comedian, or so she thinks.

"By the way, who will you test here, in this female-only zoo?"

"I know, I know, men are as scarce as . . . as meat. No, worse, as snow! Really, they should hire a few more male teachers. Just for us to look at, at least."

"You can count the men here on one hand, and even these few don't really count. Let's see, Mr. Karugonjo, who is about, what, fifty?"

"With gray steel wool for hair and the shuffle of an eighty-year-old. Thank God he is taken!"

"What about Mr. Dawan?"

We burst out laughing again.

"*Kyoka*, Nassuna, you're not serious. The poor Indian? Have you seen the way he walks? I mean, who cut off his bum?"

Mary stood up to demonstrate, pushing her bum in and her hips forward and sliding across the floor. We almost died of laughter. Girls did that to poor Dawan as they walked behind him from class. They exaggerated his walk and then fell into giggling fits, hands over mouths, fingers pointing. *Bambi*, I pitied him, even though I laughed too. What was he doing here all alone? How come he didn't leave when Idi Amin kicked out all the Indians years ago? He must have been quite young in '72, no more than a teenager. Was he a citizen or what? For us girls, he was just a laughingstock.

"Rosa, he would be great for your experiment; you could find out if African witchcraft works on Indians."

Mary followed. "Next, you could try it on Miss Straw. A white *and* a woman." We howled and rocked back and forth as if in pain.

"You people, please! Stop being silly. I'm serious. I don't think Dawan is a prime candidate for my experiment on the honored traditions of our ancestors that you have been taught to call 'witchcraft,' okay? Now control yourselves. Who's left?"

"How about the men on the farm and in the dining room," Mary suggested with a faint sneer.

"What if the experiment works, what would I do with one of them?"

"Oh, and what exactly are you planning to do with any other 'suitable' man, may I ask?"

"At least it should be someone I can *talk* to."

"Why are we wasting time?" Nassuna butted in. "We know who you want: Mr. Mukwaya, the Wodo himself. You want us to say it for you, don't you?"

"What! No, of course not. But yes, Wodo is the only suitable one."

"And your first choice, admit it."

"The only logical choice. Haven't you seen how he is in class, completely taken up by *King Lear* or *Devil on a Cross*, or whatever we're reading? It's impossible to tear him away from his first love, literature."

"Oh, you're jealous of books!"

I ignored Nassuna. "If the spell can distract someone like him, then it can work on anybody, don't you see? We would get husbands just like that!" I snapped my fingers.

Mary was now utterly disgusted. "Husbands! You've never even had a boyfriend and you're talking about husbands!"

Not Nassuna; the word "husband" made her salivate. "Hmmmm. But, the power to excite a man is not the same as getting him to marry you."

"This would be the first step. *Then* you simply refuse to give him what he wants, see? You make him suffer and plead until he is almost crazy and has nothing else to do but propose." Wasn't I brilliant?

"This is the most stupid and . . . *pathetic* idea I have ever heard. Are we going to finish with the Songhai Empire tonight or not? We've wasted enough time." Mary was no longer amused. Her strict and sensible side was never far away, and she always chose the best moment to ruin our fun.

Nassuna and I groaned. "Songhai?"

"It's too late to get back to books; let's continue tomorrow, please?"

Mary gathered up her books. "You two just aren't serious," and huffed out of the room, as if she hadn't been laughing with us just moments before. I swear, she'll end up like one of these rock-hard spinster teachers here if we don't keep working on her.

I didn't wait. The very next day I was ready with my plan. Our heavy green H.S.C. skirts have two big front pockets. I found a medium-sized safety pin that was keeping up the hem of another of my skirts, removed it, and slipped it into my pocket. Our last class that Wednesday afternoon was literature. Afternoon is when time moves the slowest because the heat makes us sleepy, especially if we've had something starchy like cassava for lunch. Our classroom is nice, though, with large open windows on both sides that let the cool breeze sweep through. The welcome distraction of bumblebees, flies, millipedes, and such, which we make a big fuss about, pretending to be frightened, helps use up chunks of class time. Also, there are tall jacaranda trees with overhanging branches on either side of the building, so it's mostly in the shade. When in bloom, the trees throw perfumy purple flowers into the class. I sit near the windows because it's like sitting outside right under the trees. A window creates space for the mind to wander; you can stare at the sky, the farthest thing ever, and think of nothing, especially during economics.

That day, if all went as planned, I would save us all from *King Lear*. If the trick worked, that is. The spell, I mean. In class, before I sat down, I put my hand deep into my pocket and curled my fingers over the safety pin. My pocket was beneath the desk; I could move my hand without anyone noticing. As we waited for Mr. Mukwaya, I wondered what I should think about as I concentrated on him. His nose or eyes? Love songs? When he walked in, my heart gave a little thump; would I be able to go through with this? I had not told Nassuna or Mary because I knew they would fidget and giggle and spoil the experiment. I didn't want to get caught, of course, but also, everything had to be as normal as possible so I could be sure that any change in Wodo was caused by the spell, nothing else. I should have studied the sciences, chemistry perhaps, don't you think?

My hand warmed up the thin piece of metal, and then it got wet; my palms were sweating. I hoped Mukwaya wouldn't notice any difference in me. The best thing would be to start the spell-study, or whatever it was, when he was deeply immersed in the play. We were at the point in *King Lear* when his two older daughters are spiraling deeper into evil. Act 3, scene 7. We called Goneril "Gonorrhea," and Regan "Reggae." God, what evil women! Mukwaya says the best way to feel the poetry of Shakespeare's language is to read it out loud, so he picked three girls to take on different parts. They cleared their throats and began. Some of us followed, reading our copies, while others merely looked down, lost in their thoughts. This scene actually is interesting, horribly so. Goneril stamps her heel into one of Gloucester's eyes and Regan does the same to his other eye. As if this is not enough, one sister stabs a servant who tries to help Gloucester. Can you imagine? Some of us giggled in shock; it was too much. After stumbling over mispronunciations, "thees," "thys," and "therefores," it was discussion time. I was ready.

Mukwaya asked, "So, why were some of you laughing?" There were more stifled giggles, shifting in seats, then silence. Now, since everyone was looking up at Wodo, I too could stare directly at him. I realized it wouldn't be enough to concentrate on his wide shiny nose, which took up most of his rectangular face. I had to look directly into his eyes. Mukwaya pressed on. "Come on, you can tell me what you think. With art, true art, there are many ways one can respond." He always talks about "art, true art, real art!" No one is impressed. Well, maybe I am, sort of. The others exchange bored looks and turn down their mouths. To help Wodo out, I started to put up my right arm, hesitated, then put up the left. I hoped no one noticed.

"Well, Rosa?"

"It's sort of funny; I mean, how can these two princesses act like this? It's . . . it's, well, not primitive, but . . . no, in fact, it *is* primitive and hard to believe."

Mary added, "Imagine. They are in a castle, dressed up in fine clothes and all. Couldn't they take Gloucester to court or something—"

Another girl, Dorcas, interrupted, "—Or at least get their *servants* to hang him, shoot him, whatever." We all laughed.

Wodo waved us down. "Well, then, we have to ask ourselves why Shakespeare wrote such a bloody, graphic scene. Don't you think he knew what he was doing?"

After a pause, a few hands went up. "Yes, but—"

"Even Shakespeare can write badly."

"Maybe he loved violence, some people are like that."

"People in power, mostly." That was Nassuna. The others murmured agreement.

I was busy rubbing the moist safety pin, softly at first, then harder. I looked into Wodo's eyes. No change. I kept on rubbing, but the mistake I made was not joining in the discussion. I am vocal by nature; those who know me know I cannot keep quiet, especially not in literature class. But I was concentrating deeply, repeating to myself, *stare, stare, stare.* God, I hadn't realized how often one blinked. But something was distracting me. I felt eyes on me on my left. It was Nassuna. She sat next to me, and had turned to me after her comment. She must have noticed that I hadn't reacted at all; no nod, no laughter. I refused to return her look of curiosity. If I gave her even just a quick glance, she would read me and guess something was up. She knew me too well. Focus, Rosa, focus.

Wodo now was answering Dorcas. It was hard to keep staring into his eyes because he kept shifting his face. When he turned my way mid-sentence, I started to sweat. It tickled my armpits. I was dying to scratch, but it would be awkward with my left hand. I did anyway, quickly. Focus, Rosa. On what? I didn't know his face was so pimply. I wished I had a chant or something.

Nassuna nudged me. I ignored her. She nudged harder. I wanted to strangle her. There was no way I could continue. I turned and gave her the most irritated look I could. She frowned in question. Annoyed but resigned, I slipped my hand out of my pocket and showed her the safety pin in my open palm, below my desk. Nassuna breathed in sharply and widened her eyes. She gave me a shocked look, glanced up at Wodo, then back at me. Her face broke into a wide cheeky grin as I slipped the pin back into my pocket. Thankfully, she had the sense to hide her giggles in her copy of *King Lear.*

I mouthed, "Leave me alone," and turned back to Wodo. He was looking at me. Had he seen us? I wasn't going to give up so fast, but I knew I should say something about the play before he became too suspicious. "Um, this is not real life; it's drama. It has to be dramatic." Okay, I admit, this wasn't my best idea ever.

Nassuna came to the rescue. "I agree. The scene is exaggerated to provoke the audience. Then everyone can feel great pity for Gloucester even though he has acted like a fool. The same goes for King Lear."

Some girls protested, "Eeeeeh, no!"

Wodo raised both hands, palms open, to stop us. "Please. One by one."

Dorcas again. "There are other, more believable ways to make us feel pity. The action here is too extreme, too cruel for words!"

Wodo wrote "catharsis" on the board, and went on to define it. I knew he would go on for some minutes; it was time to try again. This time I would do it, I had to. He talked, I stared, he talked, I stared even harder. My eyes seemed to glaze over. His face expanded, his eyes became glowing black orbs. Still, I rubbed the pin furiously. There was a soft giggle beside me. Nassuna again! God, why couldn't she control herself? Forget her. I decided to imagine Wodo . . . kissing, yes. Not me, of course, no way. Kissing Miss Bakunda. She had finished Senior Six last year, and was back here teaching SI. until her university classes started in September. I could see her having an affair with Wodo. Like I said, there was no one else here.

Okay, so Wodo and Bakunda were kissing. The more I concentrated, the wetter my armpits got. Sweat now trickled down, my blouse was damp. The staring, Wodo's deep drone of words, my own nervous heat, *something* was making me feel woozy, but I didn't dare shake my head to clear it. I felt the girls around me fidgeting. What was going on? Concentrate, ignore them, *concentrate*, I repeated desperately. Had Nassuna let the other girls know? Oh God, no! Focus, focus. I couldn't stop now. With my free hand I wiped drops of sweat from my forehead. I could see Wodo and Bakunda, mouth to mouth, he had her in his arms . . . he bent her over, oh what was he doing! I squealed.

Wodo stopped talking and looked at me, then moved his eyes from face to face. I was transfixed. I couldn't stop staring at him, *at them*, mesmerized. The girls' stopped their shuffling and giggles in startled silence.

Wodo said, "Do you find my explanation of cathartic action in *King Lear* funny?" And he scratched himself *right there*! A quick move, but one I had never seen him do before. Okay, I had never watched him this keenly before, but still. Strangely enough, I too wanted to scratch myself. Sweat was leaking out of me, and yet the classroom wasn't that hot.

Nassuna, who I am going to kill one of these days, put up her hand. "I have a question."

"Go ahead."

"Do you think Shakespeare had something against the female *sex*?" She stressed the word, knowing the effect it would have on everyone. "You see, *sex*, sorry, the female sex in this play acts like men, evil men."

"You've moved on to another point, Nassuna, but let's talk about that. What about Cordelia?"

Wodo usually could handle tricky words like "sex" in a classroom full of giggling girls; he was an expert at smoothing over uncomfortable moments. But this time, I swear, he was *physically* uncomfortable. He leaned his hips back against his desk and faced us with what was clearly a false air of ease. I was still rubbing my now hot secret, my eyes glued to his face. Abruptly, Wodo stood up again, smoothed down *the front* of his pants, then half-sat back on the edge of the desk. Did I dare continue? Push him further? I confess, I could not stop. My mind and body were an out-of-control machine manufacturing fantasies. I don't know how I managed to say, in a high breaking voice, "Cordelia really isn't a woman—"

Someone added, "Yes, she is more of a child. Very innocent."

Nassuna jumped in. "You mean she is not of the female *sex*?" Everyone gasped, fighting back hysterical laughter. Wodo stood up again and shifted himself you know where! He contemplated his shoes for a second, and then looked up directly at me. "And you, Rosa, are you a child or a woman?"

Stunned silence. A bird outside yelped three notes repeatedly. Loudly. Wodo had never asked such a direct personal question before. He stared hard at me. I couldn't turn my eyes away. "M-me?"

"Well, Cordelia might have been about your age, Rosa, seventeen, sixteen, maybe even younger."

"I—I don't know."

We waged a battle of the eyes, of stares, mine shocked; had he found out? His were questioning, insistent, mocking. A come-on? No! He wouldn't. But he had just kissed . . . no, he hadn't.

What was wrong with me? Suddenly, he turned away, walked around the desk, and said, "One shouldn't say or do things one doesn't know about." His tone was both kind and menacing, but I knew exactly what he meant. The trance broke.

Tears crept out of my eyes and I bowed my head. The hand in my pocket went limp. I was drenched in sweat, which was now cold. It was difficult to breathe. What had just happened? I needed to get out of there, out into the fresh air, take in gulps of it. Fading images of Wodo and Bakunda, their mouths still stuck together, swirled in my brain then out, like dirty water down the drain. I pressed my eyes tightly shut.

The class seemed to let out a collective breath as it turned back to *King Lear*. Mukwaya chose three other girls to read the next scene aloud. Thank goodness, now I could hide my hot face in my book. I stayed quiet until the end of class; my mind just wasn't working. Finally, much to my relief, the chapel bells rang out merrily and everyone sprang up to leave. The ordeal was over. As chairs scraped the floor and voices rose loud and free, Mr. Mukwaya called out, "Rosa, could I talk to you for one minute?"

Oh no! I looked up at him, then back at my books. What would I say? Everyone else streamed out happily; classes were over for the day. Nassuna said to me, loud enough for Mukwaya to hear, "I'll wait for you right outside, okay?" I nodded and walked warily up to Wodo.

He cleared up his notes slowly, thoughtfully, notes he hardly ever referred to anyway, until the last girl left. Then he leaned one hip casually on the desk, as casual as his stiff body could allow, and said, "You know, Rosa, you are quite a good student."

"Thank you, sir." A "sir" wouldn't hurt at this point.

"*Usually* a good student," he amended. I kept silent. Praise was always a teacher's way to start criticism. But? He gazed out the window thoughtfully for a few seconds, stroking his copy of *King Lear*. I felt my armpits tickle again. Goodness, what was happening to me? I must smell by now, I thought. Could he smell me?

"You know, literature requires passion; you have to get involved, you have to care." He looked at me questioningly. "And you do care, I've always thought you do. Your papers . . . yes, *passion* is the word." He leaned his body earnestly toward me, then jerked it back in his stiff way, catching himself. He turned back to the window. Girls poured out of all the classes and down the cement paths to the dorms for tea, to Ye Olde Shoppe for *kabs*, *mberenge*, bananas. They would spend the last daylight hours as they wished, before supper, prep time, and then bed. I had been here four years already. The rhythm of the days was in my bones. I should have been outside and free with the others.

"Of course, you could end up a teacher like me." What was Wodo talking about? He turned back to me suddenly. "What was going on today?"

I took a step back and looked at my shoes. They were Bata boys' shoes, made in Jinja, the kind most of us wore. "Today?"

"You know, the giggling, the shuffling, and you acting . . . strange."

"I—I don't know."

"Rosa, I am not a fool." I kept quiet, head still bowed. "And neither are you." He wagged a long finger at me. "Don't become one."

For one queasy moment, I knew he knew everything. The safety pin burned in my pocket; could he see its shape? Should I confess everything, just say—

"Passion, Rosa. Don't waste it." He paused, then gestured at the laughing girls outside. "You young women here, you are so protected from everything. Unlike Cordelia." He smiled. "But not forever. You will be forced to grow." He shrugged.

I was confused; where was he heading? I looked out the window, wondering if Nassuna could hear us. He wasn't mad at me; that I could tell. In fact he seemed to be taking me seriously, as a person, not just another student. "Mr. Mukwaya, I didn't mean to do anything wrong."

"No one means to make any mistakes, but make enough of them . . . ," and he gave a short laugh.

"It was just a game."

He shot me an almost angry look. "A game?" Then, lowering his voice, he muttered, "A game!"

"I'm sorry." How small, how silly I felt. I wasn't even sure we were talking about the same thing. He kept his eyes on me grimly.

"My mother was already married at your age. My sisters—" He broke off abruptly and shook his head.

What could I say? "I'm so sor—"

Wodo raised his hand to cut me off. "Rosa, I think I've said what I can." He stood up, a tall solid wall, a dam against the rushing river of the future. He moved to the other side of his desk, then paused and suddenly smiled down at me. "You can go now." He turned to his copy of the play and opened it, and, without looking back at me, waved me out. "Go on."

"Thank you," I gulped and rushed out.

Just around the corner I bumped into Nassuna, who had such a worried look I giggled and took her arm.

"What was that all about?" In relief, we took the steps together, almost leaping off them. *Digi* was completely forgotten.

"I don't know. How do I know?"

"Passion? You and Cordelia? His *mother?*"

"I know! I wanted to melt into the ground and disappear."

"Do you think he's crazy? Seriously. Maybe he's read too many books—"

"—and he's stuck here, poor him, with all that—"

"Passion!" we shouted together and burst out laughing.

"You see, my spell worked." I was so relieved I couldn't stop laughing.

"Of course it didn't, silly. He didn't stop thinking about *King Lear* for one second!"

"Didn't you see how he acted funny?"

"Ya, because I said 'sex' about ten times, you fool! And what about you? You should have seen yourself, your eyes as big as eggs. Why is your blouse damp—"

"Why were you messing up my experiment?"

"I was only trying to *help* you. To get you out of hot water! He obviously could tell something was up."

"Oh no, he felt me—I mean *it*. I'm convinced."

"All that it proves is that he's crazy. Or maybe you are. Experimenting on a crazy man!"

"He thinks I'll be a teacher, he said. Stuck in a place like this, just like him. He actually cares."

"He said that? Oh God, Rosa, Walking Wodo *loooves* you!" she sang out.

"Nassuna, please! Don't be silly."

"And you looove him *to-ooo!*" She raised her voice even higher.

"Shut up! Stop it. Stop."

"This secret romance! What are we going to *do-ooo?*" She flung her arms open dramatically, face raised to the sky, and then bent over laughing.

I slapped her arm, half angry, but she wouldn't stop. I just had to laugh too. But I knew she wouldn't let me forget this; she would milk it for weeks, months. We moved on down to the dorms, weaving our way through throngs of girl-women. They stared at two Highers losing their *digi*, laughing like they were possessed. Later, no doubt, this would swell into some dirty rumor: Wodo and who? *No!* My hand crept into my pocket as Nassuna and I slowly calmed down and tried to become grownups again. I would leave the safety pin there. Why not? Not as a game, but to remind me of what he called passion. I was caught in its spell.

A Thank-You Note

Rosa

Dear David,

I can't just let this go without saying bye, to let you know I got what you gave me and I am sure it was you. I can't resist saying this: you shouldn't have! Not that it makes much difference who it was, but still. Maybe it does. Didn't you know? Is it too late to ask? Isn't everything too late? Because this slow invisible spread, like a harmless cloud from afar, has turned into an invasion of insatiable locusts, a cruel blanket covering us all.

David, my body has started to fail me, but my mind hangs on, watching, watching, like vultures circling a sick and dying animal, a hyena perhaps, as it drags its wounded, bleeding leg to some dark undergrowth to die in secret. The hungry vultures with ugly blood-red throats are up above watching me, David, circling closer, mocking me for living, for smiling, for being Rosa, the rose, as you called me. For swaying my hips deliberately, enticingly, as I danced with you, with others. For those jeans I bought that hugged my buttocks so tightly men turned to watch and whistle as I walked by. I am mocked for saying yes. I am guilty.

The vultures mock me, David, for not loving you; for not having that great romance we read about so many times until we believed it was supposed to happen, even as we mocked love as melodrama. Better to have loved and lost, right? We could have been the Romeo and Juliet of the tropics, with disease, not family, as the enemy of love. Maybe then I would accept this, as I did you entering me slowly and surely and perfectly. Accept this like all the food I have eaten, accept this like breath. The air may be dusty or fresh, but you still have to breathe, and you do, of course, until you stop.

This shouldn't come from sex. Like a pregnancy, it's so removed from the act itself. I refuse the logical connection. Ten to fifteen minutes of heaving and pushing and a whole new *other* life is created, becomes alive, real. In this case, a slow death is born. Sex *can* change your life. But, David, I still don't believe it; the vultures must be wrong. I keep repeating to myself, this is a fact, *a fact*: I am going to die soon. I wish I had the courage to die before I feel too much pain. This body of mine only worships pleasure.

David, why are you living on and on, suffering? Yes, I'll be cruel and say it: you are already dead. Remember how you used to shout out, *Onzita! You're killing me!* as we rocked faster and faster. I lived off your shameless exuberance. I'm dying because of it. Whole days in bed licking each other. We overdid it, trying to pass the point of need, to exhaust desire. I am so exhausted now. Wiped out. Dry, but still unsatisfied.

Okay, I accept: we should be dying. We are physical bodies reacting to physical truths, cause and effect. Laws of nature. This is how it should be. But what should doesn't always happen. One should have food on the table; one should not have to watch one's father being shot dead because he refused to hand over the video deck to the soldiers-thieves-kids-with-guns. The neighbor's son shouldn't have put his finger up into me when I was ten. I should have cried out loud and told someone. But when the same thing happened when I was seventeen, I should have liked it. Why shouldn't we die at twenty-three?

The knowledge of death lives in our bones. In all of us, David. Death reveals itself when your hair starts to thin out and fall off and your skin turns gray. Skin that was praised for its smooth brown softness is now patterned with scattered rash, sores that won't heal, yellow pus, itching that is no longer pleasurable to scratch, scars, scars. Your lungs sound harsh and shake you with dry coughs. Your organs, still so young, fail you one after another until you no longer can leave the hospital, except for that one last time, when you are sent home to the village to die. But not so quickly, first the liver failure, kidney failure, mysterious tumors, and of course, always, the streamy splatter of diarrhea. Your anus will never again feel the pleasure of firm feces slowly moving out.

David, there's no point in asking you this now, but after you knew, couldn't you have kept it to yourself? I know, a stupid question; most likely it was too late by then. Have I kept it to myself, this organic, terrifying secret? No. Old habits die hard.

And, let me ask also, why should you use up all your father's money in treatment after worthless treatment? Exotic drugs from Germany and India; that prophetess Nantambi who prays for a fee, dollars only, thank you. The medicine man from the Nyaka-sura area, I forget his name, who is growing rich by lying to people that his honey defies death. Honey is honey, but he charges enough to send his children to a posh boarding school in Nairobi. But people say how can you watch your child die and do nothing? So your father throws away his money knowingly because he has to do something, or they will say the miser killed his son. Why shouldn't he lose it anyway? You told me he got rich selling government equipment and land, cement, donated cars, you name it, and he got away with it. For a while, anyway. Now he is paying. Perhaps he is now buying you the *zungv* medicine that works, that no one but ministers can afford. But still, you are paying in other ways and so am I. If it was you who gave it to me. Does it even matter who gave it to whom?

Do you remember when exactly it got a name, became real? How did we first hear about it? Rumors, whispers of strange symptoms in villages far away from us. Rakai district was put on the map because of all the deaths. The rumors were messengers ahead of the steadily approaching army; warnings that couldn't protect us from the marauding attack. Before the newspaper articles and stories on the radio were the rumors, more true than any recorded event. Stories of its power spread and grew like tree roots curling out of the ground; abnormal, ugly, strong.

First, they said the women became even more beautiful, enticing, their skin shone smooth as they carried it unknowingly, gracefully, and passed it on in quick short bursts. Then they slimmed down fast and mysteriously, and in every single village began dying like flies. No, flies are harder to kill, unless they are buzzing over a succulent, bloody carcass. The flies get drunk with blood as it clots all over their brilliantly blue, delicate wings, trapping them. They are killed by what feeds them, suffocated in already dead, smelly flesh. That may not be such a bad way to die: full, fed up, drunk.

Who is going to remember all the wiped-out young women and men of Rakai? Does it matter that they were alive once? I mean, really? Then why have they disappeared so easily? "Disappear" used to mean something just as bad, once. How many are left to keep alive the once bustling collection of kiosks, shacks, and market stalls piled high with rainbow-colored ripe and rotting fruit? The dusty pink, blue, or purple-painted hotels, motels, and happy bars, with thin faded curtains blowing in the dry heat, are empty. And inside them, perhaps one or two stray travelers find relief from the hard sun in the cool dark of the Happy Hotel, Tolinda Motel, Mohamed & Sons Express Chips, small rooms filled with smells of beer and beef stew. Can you hear the babies' wails, the children's shrieks, hollers from taxi drivers and bus conductors, women laughing or calling out their wares, chicken, goats, cows, all caught in the melee? And the haze, a stifling hug around it all, tries to keep it all there, at home. Each one-street trading center, one just like the other, still exists along the main roads that snake across Uganda, but the people are missing, as if the towns have been cleaned out by war. It is a war.

What happened? They say truck drivers transported more than goods from the port at Mombasa, across Kenya, through here, and over to Zaire. I can see the action, feel the excitement as drivers stopped from town to town, met up with old girlfriends or new prostitutes, or both. Some girlfriends became prostitutes and vice versa. The truck drivers made good money, and so carried gifts from town to town: huge bunches of bananas; powdery sacks of maize flour; shirts, skirts, and schoolbooks for their various children here and there; a nice piece of *kitenge* cloth for each mother and ten tubes of Ambi to keep her face as bright yellow as a ripe banana. Imagine the hot reunion as they unknowingly exchanged the sweetest, sweatiest gift. Their crime was that they were too friendly. They were punished for spreading love around.

No one could see the link forming and stretching across the country, a tightening chain that bound everybody together. The chain later stretched north and south, too. Wherever there was any frolicking, as we used to say, that is, everywhere. A huge microscope in the sky would have shown a crazily winding necklace of the most human of connections, circling again and again around the waist of Africa. Back then, it was just like the rash it makes around the waist, *kisipi*, another early, unmistakable symptom. God, or the devil, has a bitter sense of humor, loves cruel connections. Now, of course, it's everywhere.

David, we whispered these rumors about *them*, the villagers, but didn't talk about us, did we? Now we know we are all connected: one big loving community. Back then, we thought we were different, separate from the Rakai kind; they were born suffering, after all, but not us, oh no. We were at Makerere University; we were the cream of the crop. We had dodged the bullets of Amin, Obote, all the coups, the economic war, exile and return, and here we were on the road to success. We were the lucky ones, the chosen few. No one said this out loud, of course, we just knew we were different, protected; our fate was privilege. We didn't consciously think it, but the knowledge sat at the back of our minds like a fat cat. We were intelligent, read books for fun, had worn shoes and socks to school while villagers went barefoot; we spoke proper English; listened to Top of the Pops rather than Congolese music; ate with forks, not our fingers. And, of course, we would one day leave this place to work in southern Africa, or go to Europe or America for further studies. Escape, but not by dying.

What went wrong, David? Do you ask yourself this all the time like I do? Who brought it to us? Perhaps it was the other way around. Was it already steaming in the slums of Katanga, that huge ditch between the multi-storied halls of Makerere University on one hill and once grand Mulago Hospital on the other? I'm sure you, like the other campus boys, went down to those slums to drink crude *waragi* and enjoy crude women, because you were too poor to entice campus girls with chips and wine and money to perm our hair and buy new shoes. And we campus girls were not entirely innocent either. Frustrated campus boys watched but couldn't stop their girls turning to the older, richer *mafutas* in town, or top soldiers, new ones for every regime, just like how new, prize girls joined campus every year. *Pass it on, pass it on, be generous, blind, willfully so,* was our unspoken creed.

I can hear you protest: we weren't careless; we didn't know. At least for a while. Or didn't want to know. As long as there were no symptoms, there was nothing to be ignored except what wasn't said. *Hush,* and we passed it around like village drunkards sharing reed straws steeped in boiling pots of bitter, fermenting brew. Sex as a community event, another old tradition to be shared. The one who hoarded the straw wouldn't be invited back to the beer party. Share, share, life exhorted us; there was always more to be had. Skin doesn't wear out, not vaginas, not penises. Have a good wash and you're ready for the next day, the next lay. It was like the kid's game, tip. Chase someone, catch him, catch her, tip and run for your life, unless you kept your fingers crossed, paxies. Older kids weren't allowed to do paxies, they had to run and run, or not play at all. What fun! Too much *good* fun. Do you regret it, David?

We were young, beautiful, careless, open, giving. We never talked about the games we played, overwhelmed by the fact of bodies, of desire, of willing flesh, so available, so sweet, so easy. We could do what we wanted, and did. These were *our* bodies. After the tyranny of boarding school, religious rules, and overbearing parents, we were free! We had such a lovely gift, how could we not use it? Why should we regret it now? After all, even the good ones are dying, that's the cruelty of it. Some of the prim and proper girls who got proposed to and married quickly, while the rest of us were left floating, are being killed by their husbands. All that people say to that is, men are men, *munnange*, what can you do? Shrug with heavy resignation.

Do you think about these things, David, as you lie in bed, too weak to sit up and sick of sleeping? Do you ask yourself over and over again why Nassuna slept with Kizza when she knew he had slept with Mary, whose former boyfriend, Yonah, once had a sugar mummy, one of those fat yellow Dubai women, and we all know what business they did in Dubai. Remember those blaring red and yellow shirts Yonah got from her, the fake gold rings and pointy plastic shoes? Scandal! we whispered behind his back and laughed. So, why on earth did you have that fling with Nassuna? I know, she was the "Prize of Gayaza," "Queen of the Night," and so on. Can you believe I'm still jealous?

David, I didn't tell you, but, well, it can't hurt now, can it? I slept with Kizza too. Just once. Yes, I know, once is enough. Remember the Nkrumah Ball, second year? That party where you left me stranded, said you were coming back and didn't, so why shouldn't I blame you? Kizza walked in after you left; he was looking for Mary. Had you left with her? He was kind enough to take me back to my room, all the while telling me Mary this, Mary that. I told him you had left me there, but I didn't care. I lied. In my room, we cleared a half-bottle of U.G. as we talked by candlelight. Power had gone again that night. I remember our black shadows moving along the yellow glow of the walls as we talked. Kizza was so miserable I was moved. Oh, the way he rubbed his chin nervously, looking down, so shy. The way he listened to my sob story, slowly rubbing my upper arm. What can

I say? We comforted each other. Don't they say misery loves company? Yes, and I'll tell you how he took off my blouse tentatively, marveling at my small breasts as if they were the very first he had seen. He held them gently like they were new, fragile petals. He made me like them; made me feel precious, delicate. Why should we not have made love? Is that a reason to die?

Maybe there's no point in retracing what's gone, but I will. I don't want to lose that too, David. We must remind ourselves that this gray isn't everything. Once, life sparkled. It did. Like that time, about a year later, when Mary came by to take us to the beach one bright Saturday afternoon. Remember? She already was frightfully thin. She was with her latest, Mustafa, that fat old Indian businessman. Mary told us, flatly, that the Dubai woman had died. Just that. Her rival was gone, but she would take all of us with her. Instead of fear and dread, we reacted with recklessness.

We decided to go a beach in Entebbe. I had been to Lido many times as a kid, but had my family seen me that day, they would have been shocked to death. Mustafa was our free ride, and he bought us two crates of beer and three roasted chicken. We all piled into the back of his pickup, falling on and over one another accidentally-deliberately, laughing. We sang pop songs loudly into the wind as we chased the good times to Lido Beach. We screamed to the banana trees, the wooden fruit stands with mangoes, oranges, pineapples, sugarcane, whose colors blurred into a delirious rainbow as we rushed past. We sang to us: *"This is my life!"* And: *"Take me higher."* The wind captured our voices and laughter, and carried them over the bright green hills to people we would never know, we didn't want to know: we were the center of the universe. We were fully alive and knew it. The unspoken threat made the moment sharper.

Remember how we took over Lido like kids freed from school, like escaped prisoners? We dashed straight into the cold slap of blue water fully clothed, screaming crazily, splashing one another, ducking underneath, grabbing at legs, falling over, screaming some more, our mouths full of water. We madly chased one another out, over the sand and onto the dance floor, dripping water everywhere, hysterical. As if there was no tomorrow. We guzzled beer as we danced all together in a large circle, gyrating as though possessed; we were possessed. We showed off our wares: trembling hips, breasts in wet blouses, you boys with bared chests, muscled arms and shoulders, supple hips. Back and forth, from the red and black dance floor to cool blue water to hot yellow sand, until we collapsed, exhausted, as the day darkened indigo and the heat softened.

Later, the music was slower, a heavy reggae that silenced us, its deep bass directing us to concentrate harder on our bodies, churn our hips low, low, lower, then snake up against one another. We separated into couples, moving slow, giggling. Murmurs and wet kisses. We all had our favorites, didn't we? You wanted Dorcas that day, I know, I was watching, but she was with Robert, remember? How come Dorcas has escaped all this? Anyway, you turned to me, and I accepted, why not? That night, that moment, offered itself to us.

That was one of the very last times we were all together before we abandoned the group games. That brilliant day will never fade; the light of it will hang suspended forever, after we're all gone. It was real. The sun over the bright blue expanse of Lake Victoria was on our side. We drowned ourselves in it. That day will keep us young forever.

David, it's been, what, five months since I last saw you? Did you get *kisipi*, David? Have you lost weight yet? There was deliberate irony in the way it was first called "slim," or rather *sirrimu*. I like how we mock ourselves, even as we resign ourselves to fate. How many of us city girls were happy when we first slimmed down, I wonder. Village women prefer to stay fat, of course. Have your cheekbones become pronounced, angular, even elegant? Do your eyes bulge out from a hollow face like those images of beautiful Ethiopian starvation victims? Has your skin lost its shimmer, like mine has? Has your tight kink of hair become loose and limp? Has it fallen out, exposing head sores? Are you, like many others, hiding under a cap, scarves, long-sleeved shirts, long socks in the heat? Are you cowering in a corner, whimpering like a beaten-down dog, or are you angry? I soon will be like you, anyhow, decomposing while still alive. How dare you do this to me? I must blame you, David, anyone. But what good does that do?

I thought I'd never say this, but I hope I won't see you again. I mean it. I prefer to imagine you as whole, the David I was obsessed with. The only consolation I have is that you won't sleep with anyone else again. Is that love? But what does that matter now?

Sometimes I imagine a man and woman who have hidden the signs so successfully that they become attracted to each other. In drunken recklessness, in the dark, they undress, silently persuading themselves, *someone gave it to me, so what, so what?* While they grope each other, fumbling with zips and buttons quickly like thieves, they feel the same splotchy skin on each other and shrink back in shock. They untangle themselves, pick their clothes up from the floor, and slink off, sobered, ashamed, disgusted. Or maybe they simply hesitate, breathe hard for a few seconds, then go on fumbling, caressing, pretending the skin is soft to the touch. Why not? It's too late now, they tell themselves. And so they fuck, desperate, desolate, crying as they come.

Mary was not like that; she chose to turn away from life. I went to see her just before she died. Would you believe she was more beautiful than ever before? As thin as a stick, her cheekbones jutting out like two knives, her doe eyes larger than life. Her eyes poured out what we all thought but couldn't say, what I am trying to say now. She was too weak to get out of bed. She lay there like a starving queen, delicate and regal, lifting a long thin graceful arm to ask for her basin to spit in. All her movements were slow, studied, weary. It was hard for her to talk; each sentence terrible labor. Her mind wandered, revealing only snatches of thought before she was overcome by the effort and coughed painfully, weakly. I have never felt as lost as I did in that small, shadowed sickroom, watching Mary die gracefully, watching her accept it. As if this was the logical end to her life. The point of it all. You know Mary was not religious, she didn't even go through the requisite "saved" period in high school, but now, now she clutched a purple rosary in one bony hand, and stared at picture-book drawings of a mournful blond Jesus on all four walls. His

arms, in wide white sleeves like wings, were spread out, beckon-
ing. To where?

Mary wanted to know who else had died, was dying; that was
the only news that mattered. I told her about the time Nassuna
saw me on Jinja Road and crossed the street in a hurry, refusing
to answer even when I called. Can you imagine? I mean, we were
best friends once, and it's just a disease, isn't it? No one has escaped. No one is innocent. Nassuna still looked good, though, I
must say, but she was wearing stockings, as though she had just
come back from London or somewhere. What clearer sign is
there? Mary smiled when I said this, and I saw a glimpse of her
sarcastic old self, but then she sighed wearily, and seemed to pull
a gray curtain back over her face.

As I looked at her, I couldn't help thinking, how will I die?
Surely not like this. Will I turn to Jesus at the last minute? I had
given him up a long time ago. That was too easy, I wanted to tell
Mary. But who am I to talk? Each one of us has to die alone.
Each one has to find her own way. Mary's awful beauty, her sick,
musty breath, broke me, and I couldn't stop my tears. I, who had
come to comfort her, leaned over her frail body and cried. She
put her hand softly on my head. A weak, dry, feathery hand like
an angel's, like death, and she was silent.

Silence was like another death at Mary's funeral. You did not
miss anything, David, though you were a coward not to come.
Burials are not infectious, you know. The bus ride to Kabale was
hell; maybe you wouldn't have made it. I didn't know Mary's
family was so popular, or perhaps some of the guests were after
meat and gossip. As usual, the men sat around a fire outside the

house, while the women were either in the kitchen preparing huge saucepans of meat stew and *matooke*, or were sitting on the living room floor around the coffin, keeping the body company. That was the saddest hymn singing I have ever heard, because it was so bad.

> *Nearer my God to thee,*
> *Nearer to thee,*
> *E'en though it be a cross*
> *That raiseth me.*

The words were dragged out so slow and painfully, I had to escape. But it wasn't any better around the fire outside. We sat silent, watching the fire's fighting-red glow and spark, but it failed to inspire us. Who would be next? There was nothing but the dull, meek acceptance of the inevitable. All through the two days of the funeral the cause of Mary's death was not announced. Everyone knew and whispered it back and forth, shaking their heads sorrowfully, fearfully, their palms cradling sagging cheeks. To me, they seemed to simply be making the right gestures, the expected posture. If they were sincere, why didn't they stop gossiping and just state the facts? As though whispering around it would keep it at bay. It was already there, among us. In us. It was too late. Many of us were secretly relieved it wasn't us this time, not just yet. We had a few more days, months, maybe a year to . . . to what? To do nothing but silently deteriorate?

I got so tired of the silence, David. The unnecessary shame. I should have run out of Mary's death room screaming, *Noooo!* At her funeral, I should have ranted wildly about how we enjoyed life, despite everything. What did I, do I, have to lose? I want to fight it. They say that long ago funerals sometimes turned into celebrations, and now I see why. I imagine orgies even; sex as a loud, unrestrained, mocking laugh at death. After the burial, in the dark, dark nights beyond the glow of the fires, deep in the banana plantations, with stripped-down, damp, soft stems as cushioning, men and women mourned together. They fought death by showing how alive they were, right then, in the face of it. *Let us live,* their bodies would say. *Let's make more life! More of life. We die because we have lived. The dead are always with us.* Bodies writhed together, and it was good. What better way is there to bury your dead, if not to go lustfully after life? I must *scream* against death just like I used to with life. I must live even harder.

I displayed my body once and men approved. I will do so again with burning scars, leaking sores, gray skin. This is all I have left: to die loudly, saying, Yes, I have AIDS. Let's turn around and face it.

Will you join me, shouting out loud, just like you did before?

Rosa

CHRISTINE

Tropical Fish

f

Peter always plopped down heavily on top of me after he came, breathing short and fast, as if he had just swum across Lake Victoria. My worry that he was dying was quickly dispelled by his deep snores, moments after he rolled off me. I was left wondering exactly what I was doing there, in the middle of the night, next to a snoring white man. And why was it that men fell asleep so easily, so deeply, after huffing and puffing over you? There I was, awake, alone with my thoughts, loud in my head and never ending, like a ghost train. Sex was like school, something I just did. I mean, of course I wanted to. I took myself there, no one forced me.

Peter was pink, actually, not white, except for his hair, what was left of it. It had suddenly turned color from the stress of his first rough years in Uganda trying to start his fish export business. He was only thirty-five, but to me at twenty, that was ancient. When naked, though, he looked fourteen. He had an adolescent plumpness, a soft body, almost effeminate, with pale saggy legs. His skin felt just like mine. We met through Zac, a campus friend who also worked for Peter's company. Peter exported tropical fish bought from all over the country: Lake Victoria, Albert, Kyoga, and River Nile. He paid next to nothing to the local fishermen, then sent the fish in tank loads to Britain for pet shops. Very good profits.

Zac and I were both at Makerere University, what used to be called "the Harvard of Africa" south of the Sahara, not counting South Africa, which didn't leave much else. But that was back in the sixties, before Big Daddy, Idi Amin, tried to kill off as many professors as he could. Most ran into exile, and the "economic war" did the rest of the damage. But we didn't complain; we were lucky to be there.

I was drinking Waragi in Zac's room when Peter came in one evening. I liked Zac because he knew he wasn't going to become some big shot in life and so didn't even try. Apparently he supplied Peter with *ganja*. Because of my lifelong training to catch a suitable mate, when Peter walked in I found myself immediately turning on the sweet, simpering self I reserve for men. I recede into myself, behind an automatic plastic-doll smile. Peter looked amused by the shabby room. He looked around like a wide-eyed tourist at the cracked and peeling paint, the single bare bulb, an old tattered poster of Bob Marley on the wall, the long line of dog-eared Penguin Classics leaning sideways on Zac's desk, the untidy piles of handwritten class notes. He was finishing his B.A. in literature.

Zac got off his chair quickly and offered it to Peter. "Hey, man." Zac had convinced himself he was black American. We laughed at the nasal way he talked, the slang from videos, his crippled-leopard swagger, especially for someone so short. I kept telling him, "Give up, Zac, no one's impressed," but that was his way.

Peter refused the chair and gingerly settled onto Zac's single bed, which was covered with a thin brown blanket. The *mzungu* wanted to do the slumming right. I was sitting at the other end of the bed. Its tired springs creaked and created a deep hole in the middle as he sat down. I felt myself leaning over as if to fall into the hole, too close to Peter, into his warm personal space. I shifted away and sat up on the pillow, pulling my legs up into me. Did he think I didn't want to sit too close to him, a white man? There was a short, uncomfortable silence. But with the two men there, I didn't have to start the conversation.

Zac said, "How about a drink, man? Peter, meet Christine, the beautifullest chick on campus." He was trying to be suave, but it sounded more like mockery. I smiled like a fool.

Peter turned and smiled back at me. "Nice to meet you, Christine." No teeth showed, only the small, gray shadow of his mouth. I put a limp hand into his outstretched one. He squeezed it hard, like a punishment. His skin was hot. I murmured something back, still smiling about nothing, then took a large swallow from my drink, keeping my face in the glass.

Zac reached into a small dark cupboard. Inside were two red, oily-looking plastic plates, a green plastic mug, a dusty glass with two or three spoons and forks in it, a tin of salt, and another of Kimbo cooking fat. He took out the glass, removed the spoons and blew into it. With his finger, he rubbed off a dead insect's wing stuck to the inside. "I've got to wash this. I'll be right back," and he left me alone in the tiny, shadowless room with Peter. It was my first time alone with a white person. There was a nervous, bare-bulbed silence.

Peter turned to look around the plain one-desk, one-chair, one-bed room with an obvious smirk. I wished I could open the window and let in the coolness of the night outside. But I didn't want to move, and mosquitoes would quickly drone in. It was raining lightly outside, pitter-patter on the glass, which made the small square lights of the next hall shimmer like a black and yellow curtain, far away and inaccessible. Wisps of white hair at the back of Peter's head stuck out unevenly over his collar. The light's shine moved over the bare pink hilltop of his head as he turned to me.

"So, are you a student here too?"

"Yes." Soft and shallow.

"Yes? And what do you study, Christine?" Like a kind uncle to a five-year-old.

"Sociology."

"Sociooo-logy?" He stretched out the word, and couldn't hide his amusement. "That's quite impressive. You must be a very intelligent girl." His smile was kind in an evilish, shadowed-mouth way. I smiled back, showing him that *I*, at least, had big bright teeth. There. I don't think he noticed.

Luckily Zac came back at that moment. I quickly swallowed the rest of my drink and left. In the warm, just-rained night, the wet grass and soaked ground smelt fertile. I dodged the puddles in the cracked pavement, which twinkled with reflected street-lamp light. Not that I really noticed, I was too busy beating my-self inside. You smiling fool, why didn't you say something clever? Almost walking past my hall, I wondered why I was so unsettled, even intrigued.

That weekend, Zac told me Peter wanted us to visit him at his house on Tank Hill.

"Me? Why?"

"The *mzungu* likes you." He chuckled shortly, dryly.

"Don't be silly. I'm not going."

"Come on, we'll have fun. There'll be lots to drink, eat, videos too. Bring Miriam if you want."

We went in the end, of course. Because Peter lives on top of Tank Hill, one of Kampala's seven hills, like Rome, as we were always told in class. Up there, diplomats' huge mansions hide be-hind high cement walls lined across the top with shards of cut-ting glass. Rent is paid in dollars only. Swimming pools, security guards, and he wanted me. Nothing would happen if I went with Zac and Miriam, my tall Tutsi friend, who Peter would prefer anyway, I told myself. She had the kind of looks whites like: very thin, with high angular cheekbones and jaw, large slanting eyes. And she was so daring, did whatever she wanted with a bold stare and brash laugh. No simpering for her. She even smoked in public. I was safe.

It was fun, sort of. Peter was overly attentive, serving drinks, plumping pillows, asking questions. We ate in courses brought in by his houseboy, Deogracias, an old man with crooked spindly legs attached to big bare feet like boats. Black on bright pink. Deo spoke to us in Luganda, but not to Peter, of course. As if we were at his houseboy level. Later, I told Zac and Miriam I found Deo's familiarity vaguely offensive, as if he was saying, I've seen your kind pass through this house before. They both laughed it off. "Christine, you're too much. What's wrong with being friendly?"

Peter chose *Karate Kid* for us to watch, saying it was our kind of movie. How would he know? I concentrated on gin and tonics. This was a whole world away from home, from school. The brightly painted, big-windowed house smelt of mosquito repellent from emerald rings smoking discreetly in every room. Bright batiks on clean white walls, shiny glass cupboards full of drinks and china. Everything worked: the phone, the hot water taps, a dustbin you clicked open with your foot. No need to touch. As soon as the power went off, a generator switched itself on automatically, with a reassuring low hum.

We turned off the lights to watch the movie, and Peter somehow snuggled up close to me. I pretended not to notice as I sank into the comfort of having all my needs satisfied. There was nothing to worry about. The drinks eased me. When the movie was over, the lights stayed off. Peter prepared a joint and we all became giggly. Everything slowed down pleasantly. He moved back close to me and stroked my trousered thigh up and down, up and down, gently, absentmindedly. It was soothing. I sat still. I didn't have to do anything.

Zac talked in a monotonous drone about the hidden treasures of Egypt, the esoteric wisdom that Aristotle stole, or was it Plato, and then the Egyptians forgot everything. Peter asked, "Why didn't they write it down?" and we all laughed for a very long time. Miriam got up and weaved around the room, holding her head, saying, "I feel mellow. Very, very mellow." Over and over, giggling. Peter led her to his spare bedroom that was always ready, with clean sheets, soft lamps, and its own multi-mirrored bathroom. He brought Zac a bedcover for the sofa, then took me to his room as though it was the practical, natural thing to do. It felt sort of like a privilege. The Master Bedroom.

In the bathroom he got me a new toothbrush from a packet of about twenty, already opened. "You have many visitors?" I wondered out loud. He laughed and kissed me on the mouth. "Women?" I mumbled, as he ate up my lips. I thought about the wrapping: colored blue plastic over the cardboard box, each toothbrush wrapped again in its own plastic, and lying in its own little cardboard coffin. I wanted to keep the box, but didn't dare ask; he would have laughed at me again.

I lay on the bed in my clothes. Peter took off his clothes and draped them neatly folded over a chair, pointing two small pale buttocks toward me as he leaned over. Then he took my blouse and pants off methodically, gently, like it was the best thing to do, like I was sick and he was a nurse, and I just lay there. In the same practical way he lay down and stroked me for a few appropriate minutes, put on a condom, opened my legs, and stuck his penis in. I couldn't bring myself to hold him in any convincing way. I thought I should moan and groan and act feverish, overcome by a wild rage of some sort, like white people in movies. But I was feeling well fed and well taken care of; a child full of warm milk. One thought was constant in my head like a news-paper headline: I am having sex with a white man. It was strange because it wasn't strange. He was done in a few minutes. He tucked me under his arm like an old habit, and we sank into sleep.

Peter became my comfortable habit. On Friday evenings I es-caped from the usual round of campus parties to go to my old white man; my snug, private life. No one scrutinized me, ques-tioned my motives, or made any judgments, up on Tank Hill, except Deo. He was a silent, knowing, irritating reminder of the real, ordinary world, my place in it. But when Deo had cleared up the supper things and left to go scrub his huge bare boat-feet with a stone, I was free to walk around the large, airy house naked, a gin and tonic melting in my hand. This made me feel floaty, a clean open hanky wandering in the wind. I didn't have to squash myself into clothes, pull in my stomach, tie my breasts up in a bra, worry about anything, be anything. Who cared what Peter thought? He said nonsensical things like, "You're so many colors all over, how come?"

"What about your red neck?"

"That's 'coz I'm a redneck, luv."

"I thought so."

"Come here, you!" Our tussle ended up in bed.

My eldest sister, Patti, might have heard about Peter from some-one. She was a born-again Christian, like I was once. "Saved," with too clear and rigid a sense of right and wrong. But she wouldn't say, "Stop seeing that white man." Instead, she told me of a dream she'd had: that I was given drugs by some whites. "They only want to use you," she said. I didn't answer. What could I say, that it actually was okay? Her self-righteousness made me want to go right back to Peter's.

For some reason I told him Patti's dream. He laughed at me. I heard "superstitious, ignorant blacks!" in his laugh. Maybe not, but like with most things between us, I wasn't going to try and explain it, what one can see or read in dreams. I don't mean that they're true. But we couldn't climb over that laugh to some sort of understanding. Or didn't want to try.

One weekend, Zac told me they had gone to the Entebbe Sailing Club with another girl, some young ignorant waitress or something. "Why are you telling me?" I scoffed. Didn't he think I knew Peter? I didn't like the sailing club anyway; it was practically white only because of the high membership fees and selective sponsorship rules. I felt very black over there. Zac was surprised I didn't seem to care about the other girls. Why squander feelings, I told myself. What was more annoying to me was Peter's choice of those waitress types.

Deogracias called him Mr. Peter. I asked him, after two months or more, what his last name was. He said, "Call me Mr. Peter," and chuckled. He enjoyed the lavishing of respect I knew he didn't get from anyone back home. Mr. Smithson, I read on a letter of his. How ordinary. Whenever he whined about the insects everywhere, the terrible ice cream, and only one Chinese restaurant, I wanted to tell him I knew he was lower class, Cockney, and doing much better here, practically stealing our fish, than he ever would in Britain. So he should just shut up. But of course I didn't. Our Lady of the Smiles and Open Body.

When Peter called one Friday evening, I was having my period. I felt I shouldn't go; what for? But I couldn't tell him that, not so bluntly. How could we openly admit that he wanted me for sex, and I knew it, and agreed? Over the phone, moreover? It was easier for me to say nothing, as usual. I took a taxi to his house, and he paid for it. Peter had already started on the evening's drinks with *muchomo*, roasted meat, on his verandah. A Danish man was visiting, one of the usual aid types, who Peter had just met. These expats quickly made friends with one another; being white was enough. They grouped together at Half-London, a collection of little shops lined along a dusty road at the bottom of Tank Hill. At each storefront, melting in the hazy heat, plastic chairs sat under gaudy red and white umbrellas advertising Coca-Cola and Sportsman cigarettes with the loud slogan, *Ye, Ssebo!* With all the beer-drinking and prostitute-hunting going on, it was a let's-pretend-we're-local hangout I avoided.

I put off telling Peter about my period, but felt guilty for some reason. Finally, in bed with the lights off, he reached for me as usual, but I moved away. "I'm having my period."

"What?" I had never said no to him.

"You know . . . my period. I'm bleed—"

"Oh, I see. Well—" He lay back on the bed, a little put out.

But he fell asleep pretty soon all the same. Instead of relief, I felt empty, a box of air.

That Christmas, Peter went off to Nairobi. He left very cheerfully, wearing a brightly flowered shirt, the sun glinting off his sparse white hair and pink baldness. The perfect picture of a retiree set for a cruise. He was off to enjoy the relative comforts of Kenya, the movie theaters, safari lodges, maybe Mombasa's beach resorts. He had sent off a good number of rare fish; it was time for a holiday.

In town, as Peter dropped me off, he kissed me on the mouth, in the middle of Luwum Street, in front of the crowds, before breezing away. I was left in the bustling, dusty street, feeling the people's stares like the sun burning. Who was this girl being kissed in broad daylight by some old *mzungu*? Aahaa, these *malayas* are becoming too bold. Couldn't she find a younger one at the Sheraton? One man shouted to Peter, for the crowd, in Luganda, "She's going to give you AIDS, look how thin she is!" Everyone laughed. Another one answered, "It's their fault, these *bazungu*, they like their women thin. Let them fall sick." General laughter.

I walked down to the taxi park, ignoring them. A girl like me didn't spend her time in the streets arguing with *bayaye*. I had better things to do. Not over Christmas, but he would come back. Call me when he needed me, and I would escape to the big white house, the gin-and-tonic life, my holiday. Well, campus too was a kind of holiday before real life ahead of me: work, if I could get it, at a government job that didn't pay, in a dusty old colonial-style office; wearing shoes in desperate need of repair; eating roasted maize for lunch; getting debts and kids; becoming my parents. One option was marriage to someone from the right family, the right tribe, right pocketbook and potbelly, and have him pay the bills. With my degree I would be worth exotic cows, Friesians or Jerseys, not the common long-horned Ankole cattle. But I didn't have to think about that for two more years. For now, I had my game: being someone else, or no one, for a few hours.

Peter brought me bubble-bath soap from Nairobi because I said I'd never used it before. He prepared the bath for me. Water gushed out of both taps forever. Abundance, the luxury of wasting. If you've never fetched water, known how heavy the jerrycans can be, how each drop is precious, you can't really enjoy a bubble bath. To luxuriate in a whole bathtub of water, just for you. The lovely warm green froth was a caress all over.

Peter undressed and joined me, his penis curled up shyly in his red pubic hair. He spread my thighs gently and played with my lips. I closed my eyes, shutting out everything but his careful, practiced touch. Sank, sank, into the pleasure of it. The warm water flopped around, splashing out onto the white bath mat and shiny mirrors. Peter crept up over me and entered slowly, and I thought, maybe I do care for him, maybe this is all that love is. A tender, comfortable easing into me.

I found out I was pregnant. We used condoms most of the time. I didn't say anything when we didn't. My breasts started to swell, and my heart grew suspicious, as though my belly had secretly passed on the message. When my period was more than twelve days late, I told Miriam. I couldn't tell Peter. It didn't seem to be his problem; not a part of our silent sex pact. This was personal. Miriam's sister, Margaret, a nurse, worked at a private clinic in the city. Nobody stopped me, they all knew it had to be done. I tried not to think about it. At the clinic, the anesthetist droned at me in a deep, kind voice as he injected me. I was going to remain conscious but wouldn't feel anything, he said. Just like real life. The doctor was cream-gloved, efficient, and kind, like Peter. I fell into pleasant dreaminess. Why did I always seem to have my legs spread open before kind men poking things into me? I let them.

At the clinic, I read an article about all the species of fish that are disappearing from Uganda's freshwater lakes and rivers because of the Nile perch. It was introduced by the colonial government Fisheries Development Department in the fifties. The Nile perch is ugly and tasteless, but it is huge, and provides a lot more food for the populace. But it was eating up all the smaller, rarer, gloriously colored tropical fish. Many of these rare species were not named, let alone discovered, before they disappeared. Every day, somewhere deep and dark, it was too late.

Margaret gave me antibiotics and about two years' supply of the pill, saying curtly, "I hope we don't see you here again." I was rather worried, though, because the doctor said I should not have sex for at least two weeks. What would I tell Peter when he called? Maybe I should say what happened. Now that I had dealt with the problem, I wasn't bothering him with it. I just wanted to tell him.

I went to Peter's office without calling, not knowing what to say. It was on Barclay Street, where all the major airline and cargo offices are, convenient for his business. It was surprising how different Peter was at work: his serious twin, totally sober, a rare sight for me. He got authority from somewhere and turned into the boss, no longer the drunken lover. Once, at night, he told me how worried he was because all the workers depended on him—what if he failed? This talk, the concern, made me uncomfortable. This wasn't my picture of him.

The first time Peter took me to his office, on my way back to school, an Indian businessman came in to see him. The Asians were coming back, fifteen years after Amin gave them seventy-two hours to pack up and leave the country. They were tentatively reestablishing themselves, which didn't please the Ugandan business class too much.

Peter led the short, bustling black-turbaned man into his back office, where I was sitting. The Indian glanced my way and back at Peter, summing up the situation. After a curt "How are you?" he dismissed me and turned to business. Jagjit had come to sell Peter dollars, which was illegal except through the Bank of Uganda, but everyone did it anyway, by *magendo*, the black market. He produced a thick envelope and drew out old, tattered green notes. Peter checked each one carefully, rubbed it between his palms, held it up under the light, turned it over, and scrutinized it until he was satisfied. He put aside one note, then went back to it after checking them all. He said, "Sorry, Jagjit, this one's no good." It was a one-hundred-dollar bill. That was about one million shillings.

"No, no, that can't be. I got this from Sunjab Patel—you know him—over in Industrial Area." Very fast, impatient.

"Yeah, but *I'm* telling you it's not worth anything. Look here—" and they compared it to another, straining their necks and heads from note to note. Finally, Peter picked up the false note and, with his usual smirk, slowly tore it in two, steadily watching Jagjit's face. He was too shocked to protest, his large brown eyes fixed on the half-notes in each of Peter's raised hands. Peter held the torn pieces over the dustbin and let them float down slowly into it, all of us watching. "You've got to be careful; *anyone* can cheat you around here," he said, and shrugged. Peter turned to his safe, snug in a corner, and pulled out a canvas bag, which he emptied onto the table. Jagjit counted the many bundles of weary-looking Ugandan notes. He was flustered; whether with embarrassment or annoyance, I couldn't tell. He packed them up and out he rushed, after one last look at the torn note, as if he wanted to grab it out of the rubbish bin and run. Poor him, I thought, but then again, he deserved it for giving me the once-over and deciding I didn't count.

Peter shook his head slowly. "The bastard."

"I don't think he knew."

Peter reached over and took the half-notes from the dustbin, patted them off, and laid them together on the table.

"Peter!"

He smiled to himself, then looked up. "What if I gave it to you?"

"What!? What would *I* do with it?"

"My little Christian Christine," and he chuckled.

This time, Peter was busy with a group of men who were loading a pickup parked on the street. I was startled again by the way he was at work: stern and controlling, giving directions in a loud voice, striding up and down. Then he saw me.

"What are you doing here?" Brusque and impatient.

"I was just passing by." I felt horribly in the way.

"I'm busy."

"But—I—I have something to tell you."

"Okay, okay, wait."

He waved me on into his back office. After a short while he followed. But, somehow, I couldn't say it, so I asked him for a piece of paper and biro, which made him even more exasperated. I wrote down, "I have just had an abortion."

Peter took the paper, smiling impatiently, thinking I was playing a childish game. His usual smile got stuck for an instant. A hint of what looked like anger flickered across his boyish face. He didn't look up at me. He took the biro from me, wrote something down, and passed the note back across the table. It read, "Do you want some money?"

I read it, glanced up at him quickly, then away, embarrassed. Back to his five little words. I shook my head no, my face lowered away from him, no, not money. I had nothing to say, and he said nothing back. After a bleak silence, like the silence while we made love, far away from each other, I got up to leave.

"I'll call you, okay?" Always kind.

"Okay." Always agreeing. Yes, okay, yes.

As I walked out, Peter's men moved aside in that over-respectful way they treat whites, but with a mocking exaggeration acted out for their black women. As usual, I ignored them, but shrank inside as Peter kissed me dryly on the lips, in front of them all, before I left.

The street was hard and hot. Filled with people walking through their lives so purposefully, up and down the street, so in control. But they seemed to be backing away from me. Did I look strange? Was there blood on my dress? The hot, dusty air blown up by the noisy, rushing traffic filled my head like thunder.

Did I want money? What did I want? Bubble baths, gin and tonics, *ganja* sex, the clean, airy white house where I could forget the hot dust outside, school, my all too ordinary life, the bleak future? A few hours free from myself. Was that so bad? Had I wanted *him* to care, of all people? He was trying to help, I supposed. I'm sure the only Africans he knew needed money. Six months of sex, and did I want money? What did we want from each other? Not a baby, obviously. Nothing that perma-nent. Our baby. What a joke. I discarded my baby like I did my body, down a pit latrine crawling with cockroaches.

I waded through the taxi-park bedlam into a *matatu*, and was squashed up on all sides by strangely comforting fat hips, warm arms, moist breath. The old engine roared to a start, blocking out the radio's loud wail of *soukous*. The driver revved the engine repeatedly to get passengers to come running, as if we were leaving right away, only to sit for another fifteen minutes. The conductor screamed for more, for more people, ordering us to move over, squash up, we all wanted to get home, didn't we? Hawkers pushed cheap plastic through the windows into our faces, their spit landing on our cheeks. The voice of one of them pierced through the noise, pleading insistently for me, me, to buy some Orbit chewing gum for my young children at home. "Auntie, remember the children, be nice to the children!"

We finally moved away, swaying and bumping up and down together with each dive in and out of potholes, each swerve to avoid the oncoming cars that headed straight toward us like life. I closed my eyes, willing the noise and heat and sweat to recede to the very back of my mind. The glaring sun hit us all.

Christie

vii

Lost in Los Angeles

I

I am here, but I am not. Flying on a plane from Uganda to New York to Los Angeles doesn't really take you there. The United States of America. The desert of Los Angeles, cut across by long wide strips of gray asphalt that are too smooth to be real. Not a bump is felt as you cover distance; it's hard to tell you are even moving. As far as I know, roads have potholes and car rides are often treacherous. But here, they are flat and endless, matching the hard, high, indifferent rocks scattered with small dry shrubs like mean little favors. Los Angeles. I'm trying to put my feet firmly on the ground. I'm trying to be here.

I am in L.A., not any other American city, because my cousin Kema lived here; she went back home a month after I arrived. I didn't know her before, but we share blood, so of course she opened her doors to me. Kema came to America in her late teens to study, and spent almost all her adult life here. But despite her

Americanness, I could see home in her; she shared her family's sharp wit and rather mocking smile.

On my first day in L.A., Kema took me on a drive-by tour through Sunset Boulevard, the lush mansions of Beverly Hills, the endless, flashy Wilshire Boulevard, and back to downtown L.A. to the cardboard tents, the scattered misery, trash, and desperadoes of skid row. I was still jet-lagged and fatigued after almost two days of flight from Uganda, so all I absorbed was a surreal sequence of enormous, shiny images and grayish dirty despair rushing past the car window. Kema's voice-over alternated between admiration, envy, scorn, and pity. I was stunned by the absurdly exaggerated opposites only a few miles from each other. More shaken than your typical tourist, I think, because I had nothing to compare such opulence with, however garish some of it appeared later. And I thought I knew what real poverty looked like. Skid row? In my jet-lagged state, I felt I was in a nightmare back home, because almost all the pitiful rejects were black like me. But we don't have skid row.

An image of my father fallen and mumbling in drunken slumber by the side of a street in Entebbe rose in my mind, replacing the misery outside the window. At least he had grass to fall on. My sisters and I took turns dragging him home. My cousin's voice brought me abruptly back to L.A. "See the Banyankore of here?" She warned. "This could happen to you too if you don't work hard." She switched to her American twang, "Wake up, honey, and smell the *black* coffee!" and laughed. She didn't really think someone like *me* could end up with a dirty cardboard box for a house; end up a heap of rubbish lying in the street, did she? But who had thought Taata would end up the way he did? That was the end of his dream. This was the beginning of mine in America.

II

On Saturdays, with no one to talk to, I go up to the hills above Pasadena, driving through the sunlight, my familiar friend. I recognize the sun at least; it is a hot dry hand on my back. I own a car now, just like that. I have learned how to drive an automatic; it's so easy. So now I just get in and go, like any other Angeleno. Free, fast, and empty, to the base of the dusty bare hills, where I park and walk. The soil, like the sun, is familiar, although at home the soil is a deeper brown, thicker, not so flyaway. Here, I feel small stones rolling under the soles of my canvas shoes. I find myself searching for signs of home, as if recognizing the palm trees, heat, and hibiscus flowers will reassure me that I'm still on the same planet. But it would be silly to expect heavy green trees and grass that is thick, wet, and healthy. This dry gray color of buildings, road, dust, and smog has its own sad beauty. I've noticed there are no butterflies here, not even houseflies that land heavy and stinking on your face, reminding you of the living. No animal smells or wafts of dead and rotting things in the air. Only the sun: a constant that leads me sweating, up, up the hill and, thankfully, out of my head.

Once at the top, looking into the distance, I can tell where downtown Los Angeles is by the brown cloud hanging over it like a threatening storm. But it doesn't rain in L.A. The cloud of smog is an empty promise, no, a menace. But whatever it forebodes, it's too late; this is where I have chosen to be now. I cannot, will not take the next plane home.

Tired of the lonely walks, I sign up to join a walking group advertised in Pasadena's local paper. At least I'm trying. Someone must have ordered the group to wear a uniform of blue jeans, T-shirts with catchy slogans, and huge white sneakers like boats. I wasn't told, so I'm wearing a wide skirt. We walk through the same Altadena hills I've been through, but at dusk. The sun is softer now. I'm the only one on my own, so I walk behind the family groups, eavesdropping. The children's nonstop whiny voices grate on my ears. How long will it take them to become the gray-haired couple walking ahead, hand in hand in companionable silence? I envy the two, merging into one in the growing dark. May the dark hide my loneliness.

Moving at an easy pace, we reach the top. The group leader talks about the few plants that grow in this semi-desert: creosote bushes, burroweeds, chaparral. I wish people didn't always want to *know* things, to make a lesson of everything. I stand apart, trying to tune him out. He is huge, with legs like a giant in a picture book, a head like a TV, and thick, sloppy lips. He sprays a little saliva with every long botanical name he rolls out. *Pickeringia montana*. The parents prod their kids to shut up and listen; this has to be a *useful* trip.

Suddenly, in the smoky darkness among the mingling group,

fireflies appear and flicker on and off, on and off. Everyone goes, "Ooooh!" Even Mr. TV-Head and the children are silenced. Then the kids squeal and point, while the adults smile and rub their kids' hair. We watch the tiny, brilliant sparks, like difficult insights, hesitant happiness or seconds ticking, fleeting by, uncatchable. "We have many of those at home, everywhere." I am as surprised as the others to hear my own voice, which is raspy from non-use and strange even to me after a whole evening of American voices. The others turn as one to me and ask where. I am not left alone all the way down the hill as we return. The kids, especially, are fascinated. "Africa!? Do you have lions and giraffes as pets? Do you eat zebra sandwiches? Please take me back with you?" They will not let me escape back into myself. The friendliness is overwhelming. I don't want it, or do I? Like the fireflies, I cannot decide: yes, no, yes, no, yes.

I've got to make a living right away, so I get a job temping. I wade through piles of paper daily in one of the thousands of cubicles in the ARCO twin towers of downtown L.A. The black glass buildings point to the sky like fat thumbs. They are ugly but optimistic: the sky's the limit. I don't like glass that I can't see through. Dark glass that reflects back only shadow. We who work in the immense buildings are nothing but ants that crawl in and out, day and night.

I earn twelve dollars an hour, which is more money than I have ever made in my life, even with the Ministry of Public Service job I had back home. Of course, it's nonsensical to compare that world and this. What to do but spend? I buy things, which is fun. I buy and buy and buy. A car to be paid for over six years (that's painless); a new bed with a shiny gold bedstead, matching bedside tables, mirror, and a chest of drawers; a dining room set of blue metal and glass; office clothes, party clothes, barbecue clothes, disco clothes, workout clothes, nice church clothes (I don't go to church anymore, but you never know), more party clothes (in case I do start going to parties, and they look so nice, and I don't have to start paying till October, and anyway it's *my* money), casual clothes, shoes, shoes, shoes. I can get them in different colors: brown, black, white, navy, red, oh yes, I must have red shoes. Plus, what else is there to do on a Saturday morning but drive my car to the mall and try on sneakers, high heels, flats, boots? No one, as far as I can see, wears worn soles or fish shoes, that is, shoes so old they tear wide open at the front and look like gaping fish mouths. No one has shoes so old they have wrinkled and bent themselves into the shape of the owner's feet. Except the homeless, of course.

Now, with all this variety of shoes and clothes, I'll be ready for anything, when anything comes along. Oh, but I also need a stereo, radio, TV, and kitchen things: saucepans, cups, plates, and dishes. I buy complete sets with matching flowery designs. For once, for the first time in my life, everything here is mine. It's chosen by me, it's all new, and I paid for it. These things aren't my parents' or for the family, they are not hand-me-downs, secondhands, discards, oh no. Brand new. All I've got to do is give the salesperson my card, and she lets me take whatever I want. I don't have to pay until next month, or November, or next year. I can do it over five years. I could even win the lottery and not have to work at all: just go shopping. My apartment is filling up with things. They don't move or talk or make any sound. They just sit there. They make me feel full. Fed up, as Idi Amin would say. Shopping and unpacking and rearranging is exhausting. But it's necessary. It gives me something to do.

Most of the temps I work with are young, and are trying, or pretending to try, to do something else. Or they don't really know what to do except earn a living, just like me. There's a screenwriter who almost got a script made into a movie by Warner Bros. Almost. There are acting students from Pomona College, L.A. Community College, USC. An aerobics instructor who says he is just about to get his own TV exercise show. And the older faded beauty, well, she used to act long ago but now teaches theater part-time. Oh, him? He's just a loser; he isn't going anywhere. Do you see what he gets for lunch every day? French fries. *Every day*. He's definitely suicidal. All that animal fat! And what about you? they all ask, sooner or later.

"Me? Well, I've just come to the States. I won an immigration lottery, so I came."

"Lucky you! Isn't America a great country? We open our arms wide to anyone, from anywhere. Where did you say you come from? Uganda? Where's that? In Aay-frica!? No kidding! That's a long way away, isn't it?"

"Yes." Well, no. Uganda—Entebbe, to be exact—is right here in my mind; it's where I am. I'm not sure where *this* is. Los Angeles is still just a word, a pretty word for elsewhere.

Back to work we go, to read document after document on oil spills. We are on the wrong side, that of the oil company. From all the way on the other side of the globe, I am suddenly involved, and guilty too, because I am making money from the suffocation of seals and ducks and fish that floated up dead, bloated with oil. How come I don't quit? Because it could be worse. For me, that is. Skid row is my excuse.

The paperwork is endless, like a wheel turning forever. The documents don't talk, my cubicle walls are high and gray. I plan to bring in pictures, a plant, next time, next time. Maybe I don't want to feel at home. There is no need to talk except to ask for more documents. I now know more about oil production than I ever thought possible. The oil spill soaks my dreams. I am deep, deep under the cold Alaskan ocean, frozen, slick, drinking oil for a living. I wake up dead to take another bus downtown toward the brown cloud that hangs over Los Angeles. This is where I have chosen to live.

It's the small things that bother me most. My teeth aren't white, straight, and perfect, like everyone else's here. My teeth disturb people; they frown when I smile. Small children stare up at me, puzzled. Look Mummy, a freak! I imagine they've been taught not to say. I have to repeat myself two or three times; it's easier not to talk. Even black people don't look straight at me or talk, gesture, or act the way I do. I am just as strange to them. I want to ask why, but don't dare to. My skirts and blouses, are they too long, too loose, too bright and flowery, out of date? I can't do my hair the complicated way I see black women do theirs. I go to a hairdresser's, and a light-skinned, haughty girl perms my hair straight and cuts it short; a "wrap," she calls it, but I can't do it again on my own at home. So I do my usual "Maria"—hair brushed straight back—but the short spiky ends don't even touch my neck.

I enter the tall glass cage of ARCO, smile, and move, robot-like, making space in the elevator for everyone else. They smile automatically at the wall or stare at the ceiling. We are all tensely silent, as if we are all heading toward the same dull punishment. We have no choice but to go up or down. Those who talk don't seem to say what they mean and are too agreeable. Their voices stretch out every vowel to its limit and slide and slip over every hard syllable. No *t*'s, no *d*'s, too many *r*'s overemphasized. Heads move too eagerly above bodies that are stuck fast. Once I'm on my floor, I smile and try not to talk. When I do, my voice is dry and strange. I see pity in people's faces, pity or impatience. I smile at the wrong times, and people turn away. The more I try, the less sense I seem to be making. And I thought I spoke English. But I do. I speak English, everyone speaks English, but it's not the English I know. "Are you done?" my supervisor asks. "Done? How?" He rolls his eyes then raises his voice and slows down his drawl. "Are you *finished* with that file?" "Oh, yes, yes." I fumble as I grab the file and hand it to him, feeling such a fool. Everyone else speaks like they do on TV, like in the movies. I know they are real, these voices around me, but a part of me just cannot accept this. I keep waiting for the accents to go away, to become normal, but of course they don't. I'm the one who is not normal. I've heard Africans who've been here too long talk in the same nasal way; it grows on you, unbidden. I swear never to, if I can help it. Like a good colonial subject, I like to think I have a British accent, the proper one.

Luckily, because everything works and is automatic, there is less and less need to talk. My salary mysteriously enters my account; I don't need to touch money itself, or go to the bank. I find a window-like machine and punch in some numbers. They mean something: out slips money, silently, smoothly, it must be mine. I take it. At the supermarket, I don't even need to use cash; I give the person at the counter my card and she lets me take the groceries, which are all wrapped up in four or five layers of crinkly paper and packed in colored boxes with pictures as though they were children's toys. There's no need to talk to anyone. In the supermarket, everything is laid out for you; you walk through chilly bright aisles, read the labels, pick out food. The fruits and meats smell of nothing, taste of nothing. A machine tells you how much, and the person at the counter smiles mechanically. She may say, how are you, ma'am, smiling on and off like a switch, but is she really talking to me, me, or to a body buying food? The price is fixed anyway. There is nothing to argue about, nothing to say.

I swipe my card through the metal box, my food rolls down the rubber plank, is packed quickly, efficiently, and I roll it out, down to the garage, a cement cage of cars upon cars upon cars, immense and lifeless. No one drives small cars here, and there are very few old ones. Most of the cars are huge and shiny and prosperous-looking. I have a ticket that slipped out of a metal box all by itself; it knew I needed it, it knew I was there. I took the ticket and somehow a long pole rose up, letting me into the garage. The same thing happens in reverse as I leave, only this time there's a person hidden behind a glass cage. He or she doesn't glance my way, and after I've done this enough times, neither do I. I slip my ticket and a few dollars into a metal drawer, which slips into the glass cage, slides back out with change, and the long pole ahead of me rises up. Smoothly, soundlessly, straight and narrow. Metal, metal everywhere, and I need a drink.

The same thing happens at my apartment. After the wide flat perfect roads, I click my garage door open, the metal rises up, disappearing into the wall. I slip into the cement womb of the building, enter my car slot, get out, press a button. The elevator doors slip open soundlessly, then close. A metal box lifts me up, but it's so smooth I can hardly feel it. It opens again and lets me out. I wish something would go wrong. I wish things weren't so perfect. My mouth is sticky from not talking, my face sticky with silent tears. I am home. I crawl into bed and try to remember the dirty smells of Kitoro, the dark swirling mud after an hour of rain like vengeance, hard fast rain that means it. The rotting fruit and swarming flies of Nakasero market; the unkempt, uncut grass that creeps, uncontained, uncontainable, disruptive, across any kind of man-made borders. I have been torn from natural living chaos that wrapped itself strongly around our lives. I am alone and trapped in metal. I am lost.

III

My cousin Kema has left for Uganda. I live by myself now. She did a lot to help me settle in, got me my first job, and introduced me to her friends, who are all Africans. They live the Southern California suburban life while saving money to build houses back home, educate their kids, make money, live well. What's so wrong with that? They are very nice people, all shiny with cream and fatty food, and they welcome new Africans with open arms— those who are educated and ambitious, that is. In America, we are nothing but Africans: lumped together, generic, black. Our voices get whiny and nasal too, but we can't erase the African lilt. Our children are American, though: noisy, demanding, insolent, confident, and fat.

Every weekend there is a gathering at one house or another, and we talk about home. When we were there last, five years ago, ten, even twenty. We are going back for good, eventually, but not anytime soon, oh no, who wants to live with the insecurity, the rule of army men and guns, the *magendo*—black market—such a tough way of life. Here, we have grown soft and comfortable with steady salaries we can live on; why go back to desperately running around chasing deals, sweating in that dusty heat? Someone, another recent arrival (not me, I only observe, and smile if anyone happens to look my way), tries to protest. He says it's not like that anymore. That was in Amin's time, during the "economic war" in the seventies. We have been saved by *Mzee* Museveni. A political debate erupts, in which we compare the different short-lived regimes, the deadly musical-chair coups, rigged elections, and corruption scandals.

"Obote One wasn't so bad, and it could have been even better if he had been given a chance during his second regime."

"Obote Two? He was an alcoholic by then; he should never have come back!"

"No, moreover the Baganda hated him and they wanted a Muganda in power. Remember, *'twagala* Lule / *oba tufa, tufe!'* " Laughter rings out, which helps defuse any rising anger.

"Daddy?" One of younger kids tugs at her father's sleeve. "What does that song mean?"

"See, Sharon? I wanted to teach you Luganda and you said, 'It's weiiirrd.' " He imitates her accent, then laughs with the others while hugging her to him. "We had a president called Lule for a few months, and after he was removed, the Baganda protested. They took to the streets singing and shouting, "We want Lule / if we are to die, we'll die!"

The little girl continues staring up at her father, still puzzled. "But whyyyyy, Daddy?" Back home, no child would have dared interrupt adult conversation.

"Listen, darling, I'll explain it all later, okay? It's a long story."

"Darling"! I am shocked. Since when did Ugandan fathers call their daughters "darling"?

The debate shifts to whether Asians, as we call Indians, should have been allowed to return to Uganda after all these years. Amin summarily expelled them in 'seventy-two. This is always a hot topic. "Let's be honest, Amin saved us from the Asians. You can call him a murderer, a cannibal—" Loud laughter. "—What not, but he did that one good thing." The group laughs again, some in assent, some in refusal.

"But the Indians were Ugandans—"

"With British passports!" More laughter, grunts, and head-shaking.

"Right or wrong, we suffered for it. Look what happened to our economy—it collapsed completely!"

"That was because all the Europeans and so on pulled out, stopped aid, trade. What country can survive with no foreign trade, no investment?"

"Yes, yes, blame it on someone else. It's easier that way."

"But now they're back, these *Bayindi*!" another interjects.

"Ah, but now they've learnt. They are more humble, careful."

"What careful? Their money does the talking. See how they bribe the ministers!"

"Are the ministers forced to take the money? And what Ugandan businessman doesn't bribe?"

"Then the *Bayindi* are very Ugandan!"

On and on go these debates about what really matters to us. We escape our American lives on the fringe and take center stage again. At these moments we are so far away from America, we might as well be at Sophie's Bar and Bakery in Wandegeya, sitting on wooden stools out in the open, eating roast meat and drinking Port Bell beer, swatting away the flies. Or maybe up on the Diplomat Hotel rooftop, washing away the day's sweat with sundowners. It feels that good.

"Daaaaad." The child's petulant cry swiftly brings us back. We are here in America, and we all need our reasons to stay, despite our vows not to die here, oh no! Alone in an apartment where your body may rot for days and no one will miss you? Here, where no one knows you even exist? Imagine ending life in a retirement home, where you have to *pay* someone to look after you, as if you have no children, no family? What a disgrace! We are going back home in two years; home is home. Five years maybe. No, for us, our kids have to get into college first, you know the schools at home. When I finish my house; when I've set up my business; when I get the UN job I've been promised. That's the only way to survive, you know, to get paid in dollars. If, when, if, when, but in the meantime . . . oh, here's the food, let's eat.

We rally around the barbecued chicken, limp salads, meat stew and rice, *posho* made with semolina flour. It's the same food every time; not quite home food, but close enough. It's better than sandwiches or macaroni or some other fake food, and so we eat. The talk subsides to contented murmurs and grunts of appreciation. Afterwards, the women clear up, bustling up and down, their big hips swaying heavily with each move, as purposeful and confident as the huge swathes of bright-colored *kitenge* wrapped around them. What a warming sight to see. I don't help much; I prefer to watch. But the single men take note and cancel me off their lists; not to mention, my hips aren't big enough.

My cousin, trying to help, makes a point of introducing me to the single men. Most look more polished and confident than they would have back home. Their dark coffee skin glows with health, their hair is neatly cut in a short, square "fade," they have on the right casual, loose-fitting jeans, sandals, and brightly patterned African shirt, and are armed with a degree, of course. I see fierce ambition rising like two horns from the top of their painfully neat haircuts. Their agenda for success is not complete without a wife. She had better be a good, no, above-average woman.

Kema pulls me over and warmly tells Bosco, Katende, or Wilberforce, "This is Christine, my cousin, she's just arrived."

"Oooh, you're welcome." A moist, limp handshake, a mere slipping in and out.

Him: "Christine who?"

Me: "Mugisha."

"Is it the Mugisha who was minister in Obote Two?"

"No."

"Ohh . . . which one?"

"We aren't known." Why am I being so rude? His smile stiffens, but he tries again.

"Where are you from?"

"Entebbe."

"Mugisha? Entebbe . . . ?"

"We're from Ankole." I should say I am Rwandese or from the north, Madi, and watch him disappear like the wind.

"Oh, I see . . . so you must know the Mutembes, don't you? The ones of Mutembe Plastics?"

"No."

Mr. Eligible Social Snob is fed up. His eyes rove around the room, he's thinking, "Next!" Luckily my cousin, who is as smooth as butter, eases him away. I should tell the next one point-blank: "I'm a nobody." Being just me, an individual, is meaningless, which may be what I am escaping from. And yet, who, what am I separate from my sisters, my extended family, the schools I've been to: Gayaza, Makerere; my religion, my clan, my tribe? That's what I don't know.

But at least I can drink and dance. I'm not used to the strange upside-down effect of these afternoon rather than night parties, with the sun and heat still shimmering outside. But what else do you do after eating, after covering all the usual topics of conversation, now that a few beers or whiskies are swimming in your blood? You dance. The music is turned up, but it doesn't seem to bother the kids, now sprawled out over the carpet and seats half asleep, exhausted by the attention and excitement and too much food.

The fast, syncopated, guitar-energized Congolese music is another way to go back home. It's a relief from battling the alien world that envelops us the minute we step outside our doors. We cluster together and dance to break away from the self or nonself we have to be at work, among foreigners, in the white world (even though there are blacks there). It's a difficult act, a tiring one. So why not let the wails of *lingala*, well-known oldies played again and again—Franco, Papa Wemba, Kanda Bongoman—

why not let them take us back to that safe, *known* place? Sure, we left it willingly, and it wasn't heaven. Now it seems like it was.

We know the *dhombolo*, we love doing it together, churning our waists and hips, arms flung up in the air as if this will save us. But I tire soon. Some of us ("*Oba*, who do they think they are?" I imagine the others thinking) danced more to *zungu* music than Congolese hits back home. Black American hits actually, not white-*zungu*: Michael Jackson, Kool and the Gang, the Commodores. To be honest, my nostalgia is largely borrowed; that's why it doesn't last that long. Their memories are not mine. Perhaps I haven't been here long enough to feel African. I admit, I am not entirely comfortable with the idea that these Ugandans, and Africans in general, are more *me* than anyone else. I didn't even know these people here when we were back home. How can I, in fact, *why* should I feel one with them, or with any African, here?

After a month of weekends at these afternoon parties, I am sick of this game of going back home. I have just arrived; I want to be here, in Los Angeles, in America, whatever this means. To try and crack this new code if I can. I left home for a reason. I will try and find out what that reason is.

IV

I must get out of my apartment on Saturday. I must. I dare myself to go alone to a club in Pasadena to listen to a live band called Sweet Poison. It plays punk music, whatever that is. The club is five blocks from my home, so why not? It is dark and warm inside, full of people. Many different random objects are hanging from the red walls: a dolphin, T-shirts, guitars, old photographs, license plates, wheels. One would think a hurricane blew through and stuck objects haphazardly, precariously up on the wall.

The band is all white, with long shaggy hair. They aren't dressed up at all, but rather wear T-shirts and baggy pants in ugly gray and brown colors, as do most of the crowd around me. Even the girls. They all must have just crawled out of bed and walked in. I, of course, am decked out in tight green velvet trousers and a frilly white blouse. I feel like a fool, even though it's now so normal for me to be in the wrong place and to look wrong. What does it matter anyway? There is no chance on earth anyone I know will see me. No one here really looks at me; avoiding strangers' eyes seems to be the polite white way. It makes me feel like I don't exist.

The band is much too noisy, but I stay anyway. I lean on the wall and watch the band scream and gesture wildly, while the crowd stands stock still, beers in hand, or hands in pockets, and simply watches. There's no obvious reaction, no dancing. One or two guys nod to the music, their hair jerking back and forth as if they're receiving electric shocks. That's it. Are they having fun? My beer heightens the absurdity of it all, and I giggle, covering my mouth with my hand. I could very well be on Mars. All the same, I'm out by myself, and so far I'm okay. I haven't been raped or anything; I'm not even noticed! I go home, take off my smoke-filled new clothes, and decide to be an amateur anthropologist, if nothing else.

The next time I'm back, the bar is just as crowded with hairy people. One of them, I can't tell if he is a man or a boy, is squashed next to me along the wall. He is very tall, thin, and loopy. I imagine his bones would make useful tools or musical instruments. His long hair, in disarray, hides his face. Its many sandy colors make him look like a friendly shaggy dog. I wonder if the hair is heavy. Should I ask? He looks ungainfully employed, as if he simply obeys the wind. He wouldn't try too hard at anything, except maybe at telling a good joke or choosing a good beer, or jerking off. I've traveled halfway across the world on my own; surely I can talk to a stranger. The loud racket from the stage helps silence my mother's shocked reply, and my drink urges me on. I sway slowly from side to side. The more I listen to this hectic noise called music, the better it gets. Its clangy, chaotic brashness is refreshing somehow. I'm wearing jeans this time, but they're still too new, a bright blue, and I cannot bring myself to go out in a T-shirt. It's okay, Christine, it's okay.

Shaggy-Hair's elbow knocks my shoulder. I turn, and he says, "Excuse me."

"What?"

He leans down like a swinging vine and shouts in my ear, "Excuse me, I said."

I'm not sure which "excuse me" he means. "Yes?" I shout back, my head turned up to him. We're both still swaying.

"I knocked your shoulder. Accidentally." He does it again to show me.

"Oow!"

"Sorry." His bushy eyebrows are busy working across his face.

"You did it again."

"I know. I said sorry!"

By this time I'm giggling. "You're not sorry, you did it on purpose."

"Yes, I mean no, not the first time. I've got long arms, see?" and he spreads them out on both sides. They stretch across my face, smelling faintly of soap and smoke. There is a visible lack of muscle. Maybe he reads books.

"Where are you from anyway? You have an accent."

An accent always helps; it's an obvious opening line. I shouldn't complain. "So do you."

"What?" he leans further down. His falling yellow hair tickles my cheeks.

"Africa." I no longer say Uganda; I'm not paid to give geography lessons.

"Cool."

"It's quite hot, actually."

He laughs. "I meant, 'cooool,' you know," and gestures, spreading long bony fingers. He apparently likes to talk. I hope he doesn't ask what I'm doing in America, as everyone does. Can't I just be here? Be as purposeless as anyone else? Luckily, he prefers to talk about the band, so I just listen and enjoy watching his spider-busy fingers and his eyebrows wriggling like furry caterpillars up and down his face. I nod and smile and drink more beer. This is progressive music, he tells me. I say it doesn't sound like progress, and that gets him going, giving me a brief history of rock and roll. The band stops, the room clears, and we move to the bar for more drinks.

Robert, or Raab, as he calls himself, has traveled to Jamaica. That's the closest he has been to Africa, he says. I tell him I feel like I'm on Mars here. He says, yes, Los Angeles is weird, isn't it? He's from Philadelphia. I don't think we're talking about the same thing: East Coast, West Coast, it's all the same to me. His face is so strange, maybe I *am* on Mars and *he* is the alien. I giggle. The flirting moves into high gear. Raab calls me brave for leaving home alone, coming to a bar by myself, and I want to believe him. I tell him he must really be so strong, with all that hair, like Samson. He hasn't read the Bible. We continue talking, each of us about different things; two separate, parallel conversations, but we're trying, we're willing.

Raab says he likes my large lips, and instead of replying, "Everyone I know has 'large' lips," I say, "You can have them," and we kiss. It's even easier, smoother, after that. Really, I think, as we explore each other's face, men and women don't have to talk; we should just rub faces, eyebrows, noses. Sniff each other like dogs. We do, and end up in his bed (an especially long one), panting and entangled. His long, hairy legs and arms are everywhere, under and over me; it's like I am making love with an octopus. A warm, furry, active, attentive octopus. I remember an old TV cartoon of a one-octopus band: it played all the instruments, its tentacles wriggling gracefully everywhere. I tell him. He laughs and winds tight around me. I bite his large nose gently, smooth his eyebrows, hold on to his long abdomen. Here I am, mind and body together, in this boy's bed, in Los Angeles. This is new. Let me turn away from the past. I'm so tired of it.

Raab is friendly in the morning, as if it's perfectly normal to wake up with a stranger, an African woman who is hungover and silent, in your bed. He offers me breakfast, but I don't want to eat anything—maybe some coffee. He gives me aspirin and juice and is casual and sweet. We exchange phone numbers, and then he drives me home in an old Volvo his parents gave him. "Take care," he says, kissing my cheek. "Of what?" I ask. He laughs, and waves his large hairy hand.

That week, I feel loose and happy, and it shows, because I actually laugh at work, a real laugh. The distance between the others and me seems less, somehow. They too sense a breaking down, I guess. Another temp, Ta-Mara, invites me to lunch. I find I am less on edge about the usual "Africa" questions. Sex heals some wounds, apparently. Ta-Mara's from Washington, D.C., and has just finished college. She's going on to grad school, maybe. That's what her parents want. She says she is postponing real life, here in Los Angeles. I tell her I left home to escape real life. We laugh. "Well, you came to the right place: La-La Land," she says. We all talk about Los Angeles as if we aren't really here; as if it lacks physical solidity. The desert was dreamt away, and now here we are, not grounded. Floating.

Venturing farther is easier now. I learn about poetry readings in the *L.A. Weekly* and I wonder what that's all about. They are held at a coffee shop in Old Town, Pasadena, which also is close to my apartment, so with my newfound faith, I go one Wednesday night after working out at the gym. I have joined the army of those who insist we can and will reshape our bodies, who cares what God intended? Aerobics is fun, it's dancing really, the music is funky and fast, and small talk isn't too hard with naked women strolling casually around in the bathroom, their breasts drooping nonchalantly.

The energy after exercise makes me feel like a conqueror as I drive to L.A. Café. It's a narrow, drab, bare-brick room lined with old couches. A few metal tables and chairs in the center face a small podium. Near the entrance is a plastic counter sticky with spilt tea. A young girl who looks like a starvation victim, with sharp white sticks for arms and black shadows under her bulging eyes, stands behind it. She wears a dog collar and stares at me silently, intensely. I timidly ask for tea. She asks what type, waving her arm behind her to the rows and rows of tea jars. I cannot read the labels so I say, any. She sighs heavily, then with effort asks, regular or herbal?

Regular meaning what? "Um, maybe, herbal."

She rolls her dark, almost glittering eyes. "Chamomile, apple, orange, mint, ginseng, rose petals . . ." I can see this is excruciating torture for her.

"Chamomile, please."

"Sugar or honey?" she asks sternly. I am afraid of giving the wrong answer, so I mumble something. She bangs down the honey jar, which is shaped like a little bear, in front of me, saying, with a voice as brittle as her twenty metal rings, "There. Honey's good for you." I dare not resist. "You must be new here," she barks. "The muse welcomes you." But why is the muse so angry?

She turns out to be the star poet, with a tragic four-line poem about her parents.

Love!
Mummy and Daddy make loud noises.
Hate!
My dog and I leave home.

After each line she pauses dramatically and stares us down. We shiver. She starts with a low rumble, screeches out the next line fast, spits out the third, and then, now that we are all hanging by a thin wire, whispers the last line. Silence.

We don't know what to do for a long moment; is she done? But when she looks at us expectantly, the anguish gone from her face, and breaks into a smile, we clap enthusiastically, relieved. She was accusing her *parents*, not us! The star bows deeply, her pale, hollow face as serious and stern as a nun's, then she goes back behind the counter. I don't dare get any more tea.

I stay longer, though, because the room is shabby, smoky, and dim, a comfortable hiding place to watch others, and to dream myself onto the stage. There are the same kinds of shaggy-haired young people here as the ones at the club, but they are dressed more colorfully and crazily, all in black with chains, hooks, and rings, or in long flowery skirts and what I come to learn are "ethnic" print blouses. They wear heavy black boots or ragged sandals, or go barefoot. No one looks too clean, except me, of course. What do my clothes, my face say? That I am a temp working for

ARCO, or an African, or an immigrant, an alien, or simply black? All and none of the above. Then how should I say, I am me?

But I do like these people, this cult of carelessness, because there is no way they would know anything about me, or would be able to judge me, even if they cared to. And I can never be who they are, so I don't even have to try. Nor do I want to be; there is nothing I need to be, here. Being lost is freeing.

The next Wednesday at the café, two girls come up to my table and ask if it's free. I nod, not wanting my accent to give me away, to lead to questions. I shrink into myself a little, but one of them insists on talking to me. Soon enough, she asks where I am from. "Africa" almost sends her into raptures. She is Native American, she says. Her friend, Debbie, grunts. She is fat, with bulging cheeks and narrow, squashed-in eyes. She smells of something, old food perhaps, I can't tell. The talkative one is called Light Feather, and she is suitably small, thin, and pale. One of her eyes is unfocused, the cornea moves around unpredictably. Feather tells me everything about herself, her wild eye making the story stranger than it is. She was born in Nebraska, but she and her brother ran away to California to escape her parents, who belonged to a religious cult. I look at Debbie for confirmation. She shakes her head and turns the edges of her thin lips down. Why is this stranger telling me lies? Why is she even talking to me? I thought we were here for the poetry.

Light Feather can't stop talking; no wonder she has such a silent friend. She says too many people think she's white so she has to dye her blond hair brown. Debbie grunts. Light Feather asks where I live, how I can afford to live in Pasadena, a new immigrant like me. She doesn't wait for my answers, but keeps saying she likes how I talk.

"Your voice is like a song, do you know that? I'm sure you sing well, what black doesn't? Just like us Indians, you people are favored by the gods. That's why indigenous people suffer." Debbie grunts again, but remains expressionless. She seems to be half asleep, and wheezes like a steam engine.

To stop Feather's stream of words, I ask, "Did you grow up on a reservation?"

This time Debbie interjects flatly, "She's not Indian."

I look at Feather. She flips back her long brown hair impatiently, and raises her high voice. "People are in denial here in America, you'll learn, you'll see. I accept my past; I know I'm Native." Debbie shrugs, rolls the little there is of her eyes, and turns away. She isn't bothered enough to argue.

I say I'm leaving, but Feather insists I listen to her poems first. On stage, her thin voice strains even higher. She recites a poem about the long, strong heritage of her people. The crowd is kind; we clap like we do for everyone else, and she blushes triumphantly. Her second poem has many animals in it, including a clever coyote, a strong eagle, a spirit bear. She does a little jig, making a circle, and ends with a loud whoop. The clapping is less enthusiastic. I feel pity for her, and clap longer than I mean to.

Back at the table, Feather, flushed from dancing, tells me I must write an African poem. Americans have no clue about Africa and native people in general, she says. It's our duty to set them straight. What do I know about Africans, I only became one after I left, I think but don't say. I am a Munyakore, but who here knows what that is, or cares? Feather preaches on in the dim light, long after the poetry reading is over. The constant refrain is her people, our people, native people, evil white people. Her weak eye seems to accuse me too, and yet I thought we were on the same side! Her good eye is kind, which is even more disorienting; two contradictory expressions on the same face. Everything Feather says is mingled with Debbie's smell and heavy passivity; she sits there like a log, like a big fat old dog. What is she thinking? I interrupt Feather abruptly, and, as if coming up for fresh air, ask Debbie if she writes poetry too. She shrugs and looks away. Thankfully, this silences Feather for a second, and I grab the chance to quickly say bye. Promising to come back, I escape.

Strange, strange, strange, is all that's passing through my head on the way home and as I lie in bed trying to sleep. Remembering the star waitress, whose latest poem was about her menstrual blood, as red as a communist, I giggle and giggle until I'm laughing hysterically, alone in the dark. Thinking of Feather and Debbie slowly sobers me up. There are so many of us who are lost, so many.

That whole week I am unsettled inside. All my ways of thinking are rearranging themselves in my head. What other people think about me recedes, as I grasp for . . . for what? I decide to write a poem, to clarify things, to try, anyway. Not about home, nor Raab, whom I saw again once, but we had nothing more to say to each other. No. Maybe something about the adventure of being lost and what I can find.

The next Wednesday I am at the café early. I sign up to read my poem before I can change my mind. My palms are already sticky with sweat. On the small stage the stark light is terrifying. My piece of paper trembles to match my voice, but I read on, reminding myself: no one knows me here, no one real will ever know.

have body, will travel
through the maze of my unbelief
to the stone wall of my yearning
for more.

The applause could have been a little more lively, I think. I'm not even sure they heard what I said. My famous accent. It is a desperate poem, but that's okay, I have done it. Light Feather likes it, and when I sit back down, she strokes my back reassuringly, smiling into my face. I've learned to sit on her "good" side. She says, "Soon, you'll write about your people; the ancestors will speak through you. Your people need a voice, you know." I'm not so sure they don't have one, but in my euphoric state I agree. Later, we all go to smelly Debbie's grandmother's house, where she lives, also in Pasadena. We eat Big Macs, and then crunch granola and drink ghastly red wine.

We keep meeting on Wednesdays at the café, and then on other days too. Light Feather has a softness, an innocent vulnerability I like to be around. She really believes I'm like her. I can imagine what Africans here would say if they were to meet us together: "Surely, Christine, if you want white friends, can't you pick better ones?" That's part of her attraction. Also, she shows me I can be anything I want.

Feather walks people's dogs for a living; she says they speak to her. She lives in one small room and a tiny yard, what at home we would call a boys' quarter. She has five or six cats, I can't tell, they completely fill her wreck of a room. The cats are furry and huge, and slink or spread all over us like physical music. Their fur floats in streams of sunlight. We hike up the Altadena hills often, where we drink cheap wine, write and read poems, and shout them out to the smog of Los Angeles. Feather teaches me Pueblo chants and dances. "This is my people's land, you know," she says. "All this," sweeping her arms wide, around.

"Mine too," I say. What the hell.

Christine

viii

Questions of Home

Christine feared the plane was about to land in Lake Victoria but had just missed it by one quick swoop to the left. Looking down at Uganda's international airport, she could tell the lake was below because there were no lights at all, just a blank indigo mass. Entebbe International Airport shone dimly in one tiny area. The town's lights were scattered and weak; Entebbe was asleep. How different it was from the spread of brilliant lights that was Washington, where the night was never dark but rather a hazy yellow. Bright orbs illuminated the memorials and monuments, giving passengers a film version of the city as the plane circled up and away. Christine was glad to leave Washington, to keep only a few choice images of it in her mind. She was home for good.

Back on earth, the passengers clapped, many of them glad to be coming home. Christine clapped with them. There was a feeling of camaraderie after sitting so close together for fifteen hours, through all the takeoffs and landings of the Ethiopian Airlines

plane in New York, Rome, Addis Ababa, Nairobi, and finally Entebbe. The passengers had shared the cramped, worn seats, the
safety instructions repeated each time in English, French, and
Amharic, the tiny toilets and scary blue water, the cramps, indi-
gestion, cold, dry, stale air, and dull Muzak. Even the pretty
Ethiopian air hostesses became as familiar as sisters or maids.
The fifteen hours merged into one endless drone of a moment.
Arriving was such a relief, whatever the destination. For Christine, it was home again, after eight years.

On the ground, the passengers were asked to stay put for a
while. No explanation was given, while the crew, looking flustered, talked to one another in Amharic. Why had the plane
stopped so far from the main airport building, and why weren't
they let out? It wasn't like there was an air traffic jam here. After
about half an hour it was explained: the plane was stuck in the
mud. It was the rainy season, and even after repeated clearings,
the runway was still awash with mud. Christine couldn't stop
herself smiling at the news, her amusement compounded by the
groans of frustration around her. How perfectly third world, she
thought. It was almost too good to be true. This was the kind of
thing she vehemently denied happening when talking to her
non-African friends. The typical stereotypes of "Africa" filled her
with self-righteous anger. Well, here she was, then, about to wran-
gle with the reality itself.

The crew finally opened the plane doors, letting in the dark,
warm lake breeze. At last, the cabin was no longer a cramped
prison. The fish smell and the heat hit Christine as she stepped
off the air-conditioned plane and walked to a bus that was to

drive them to the airport building. They would have to wait some more, they were told. She had better get used to this, Christine thought. There would be a lot of waiting here, after all.

A surprise awaited Christine: the airport, which in her memory was a huge modern building of glass and large square columns of imposing cement, now looked more like an abandoned barn than anything else. Was she only going to experience expatriate clichés? This was home; she wasn't here to make comparisons at every turn. All she wanted was for her memories to become solid again, to become real physical things.

As Christine waited for her family, her body tightened with excitement and apprehension. Eight years away. Eight whole years. Christine's mother and sister Patti, who still lived in Entebbe, were at the airport to meet her. Her mother seemed to have shrunk. Her aunts had always said Christine looked like her mother. For the first time, she saw that they were right. She and Maama had the same full dark lips, a gap in the front teeth, and a long forehead. Maama was short, plump, and motherly. Christine was short too but wire thin. So was Patti. They liked to say their father gave them pygmy genes from way back when, since his ancestors had crossed over from Congo. Oh, the sweetness of familiar faces, bodies, gestures.

Christine leaned over for a hug, but Maama shyly extended her hand. How embarrassing. Exuberant Maama, whose every sentence ended with an exclamation mark, shy? They shook hands. Christine remembered that her family did not hug, as though that was too expressive. Oh, why couldn't she stop watching and simply, unself-consciously walk into her old life, become herself again? They both mentally circled each other as they gave the expected oh-look-at-you exclamations and long Runyankore greeting.

Patti stood back, smiling broadly, waiting for her turn. The sisters greeted each other in Runyankore too, but jokingly. It was their language, but they didn't usually use it. Patti then switched to Luganda, the language of central Uganda, including Entebbe, where they had grown up. *Kulika, bambi!* Finally, Patti said in English, their Ugandan version of it, "How's everything?"

Christine's mind was slower than the plane journey that had carried her body home. It would take her awhile to catch up with what her eyes saw, ears heard, and skin felt. Here was Maama, right here, no longer just in Christine's mind, a living memory, but resurrected into warm flesh. Christine had dwelt on certain physical details all these years, such as Maama's brown toes with curved pink and white nails. She had thought Maama's warm smell was hers alone, but then had caught whiffs of it on the Metro in D.C., in class, from one or two women she had passed on the sidewalk. Christine had turned around quickly in surprise, not even fully conscious that she was looking for someone thousands of miles away. Later, when she caught that sweet, slightly tangy scent again, it reminded her of those first jolts of recognition, rather than of Maama herself. Now, here they were, in the same room.

Was Christine ready? She felt like a cardboard copy of herself. Strangely enough, this was exactly how, in certain flash moments of awareness, she had felt in America. Like a Ugandan doll. An actress dressed up for the part. This fakeness soon became normal. Thank God all that was now over.

Patti was all practical help, showing Christine where to go, collecting her three matching sets of green suitcases. The rest of her belongings were coming by cargo. Since Christine was home for good, she had brought as much as she could, including all she thought she couldn't get in Uganda. "All these suitcases, *bannange*! As if you didn't live here before with what we have," her sister gently scoffed.

Maama took Christine's side. "Why can't she have the extras, for a while at least, until she gets used?"

"Yes," answered Patti. "Until she 'settles down.' Emphasis on the 'down.' When your American shoes have no soles left and your American suits are tattered." She laughed.

Christine knew she didn't really need all this stuff, but still had bought lots of organic decaffeinated coffee, apricot and peach bubble bath, pink women's razors with aloe and vitamin E, and enough lubricated, ultra-sensitive, extra-strong, non-expiring latex condoms to last anywhere from two to six years, depending on male availability. That was wishful thinking, of course, but she had bought them anyway. She smiled now as she remembered the drugstore clerk in D.C. counting the packets, her eyes bulging with shock. For a school, Christine had murmured. Luckily, she was too dark to blush.

Outside the airport building, the warm indigo air was a light embrace. "How dark the sky is!" Christine leaned back to take it all in. The sky was spread open like an endless scroll, the stars mysterious yet meaningful writing. "Just look at all those stars! You can actually see the stars!"

Maama and Patti looked at each other and laughed. "*Ahaa, nga* you're romantic these days," Patti said.

But Christine couldn't help herself. "And that . . . oh, I remember that perfumy smell . . . what is that?"

"Maybe those flowers over there, the pale blue ones, lilacs?" Patti pointed to a large bush whose delicate flowers glowed faintly in the dark. Their sweet smell wafted by again with a change of wind.

"I hadn't even noticed," Maama said. "Yes, they do smell nice."

"Nice? Not *nice*." Some other *new* word, Christine thought to herself.

The road from the airport had only one army checkpoint, which was quick and businesslike. Patti said there were now almost no demands for *chai*, no threats to dodge by secretly slipping money into soldiers' fists. The roadblocks weren't even permanent like they used to be. Christine could not imagine not being scared. No starving-thin, red-eyed, angry-looking soldiers with harsh voices? Army men who never smiled? No more repetitive, insistent interrogations meant to intimidate rather than to get information?

Christine held her breath out of old habit, but was pleasantly surprised by the friendliness of the soldiers, the casual way they swung their guns. They greeted Maama respectfully, then joked with her. The soldiers actually *told* them they were checking for drugs or other smuggled goods, and apologized for the inconvenience!

The road from the airport passed along the lakeshore for about a mile. The air was cool and fresh across her face as she looked out at the dark expanse of Lake Victoria. The car did not drown out the roar of the waves completely. How calming. Physical things remained the same, or at least it seemed so. The lake was Entebbe, its waves would always slap against its shores, whether she could hear them or not. Here she was, driving home with her mother and her sister. Christine sighed deeply, enjoying the silence. She was home.

Christine planned to live with her mother for a few months while settling in. She had left Uganda after graduating from college and working for three months. But she could not turn down the approval of her application for an American visa, even though she had a good government job. Her plan was to do a master's in public administration then come back, but she had stayed on and on in Washington, D.C. Her mother, especially, had not been happy with her "delay," as Christine called it. She wouldn't admit that America had begun to feel like home, albeit a strange one. She could not dare say she might want to stay in the States for good. African immigrants didn't do this. Home was home. She didn't even admit to herself that she might remain in the U.S., as though this was a betrayal of some kind. It was easier to postpone the decision.

What changed? The painful end of yet another affair and President Munino's call in one emotional month. One year ago, the Ugandan president had visited the States and, among other official meetings, gave a wonderful, rousing speech to the Ugandans in America Association meeting in Washington. Munino pleaded with all the "brain drain" Ugandans to go back home and help rebuild the country. They were the cream of the crop, he said; they were desperately needed. After all, he argued, most of them had been educated in government schools, and had got a free university education at Makerere. Surely going back to rebuild Uganda, now that he had established security and the rule of law, was the very least they could do. Why stay in America cleaning toilets, the president admonished. Why live as second-class non-citizens, unwelcome aliens facing racial discrimination *and* snow? Laughter released the tension built up by the accusations wrapped in praise. Their parents and the new generation needed them, Munino urged, wagging his finger sternly. Uganda was theirs!

Tears welled up in Christine's eyes as they all stood up and gave the president rousing applause. The speech made Christine feel so good, so necessary, heroic even. Before this, she had scorned any kind of nationalistic fervor; if she felt any allegiance at all, it was to her ethnic group, the Banyankore. That was who she was. Uganda was a made-up idea forcing itself, rather unsuccessfully so far, into a country. But listening to the president's speech as a foreigner in America had turned her religiously into a Ugandan.

Christine applied for an administrative position with the Uganda Human Rights Commission, under the Ministry of Justice. She asked the Commission Director to support her application for grants to help her move back. He did, and she was awarded a grant from the Ford Foundation for her salary, housing, health, and other costs for two years under a managerial skills program. Christine did not ask herself if she would have returned home without this money. She had every right to it, she reasoned, and would live cheaply in Uganda—well, relatively cheaply. The grant would have gone, if not to her, to some expatriate who most likely would live like a king compared to ordinary Ugandans. In any case, the decision was made, and here she was.

A month later, Christine started work. She took a minibus, what everyone called a *matatu*, from Entebbe to Kampala. The early morning ride on her first day, through fresh new air, thrilled her. Her fellow travelers were shiny with Vaseline and hair oil. Their shoes were so highly polished you'd think they would never be defeated by the dust. The women wore dresses of a metallic sheen that apparently were still in fashion after almost a decade. The *matatus* were no longer squashed to the breaking point with passengers like they used to be. Now they sat only three to a row, with enough maneuvering space. Back then, the whole length of their bodies slid up against total strangers as they bumped and shook their way to the capital. This intimacy, which had been natural to Christine, was something she now dreaded. She had learned in America to cringe at the touch of strangers. Now that more *matatus* meant more space for everyone, the ride back home would at least be bearable, when she would be sweaty, tired, and longing for privacy.

The taxi ride gave Christine half an hour to look ahead at the day calmly, make plans, and think nice little expectant thoughts. She would not worry. Her new boss, Mr. Musozi, had been very helpful, if rather scatterbrained, by phone and fax. She was sure she would do a good job. By the time the *matatu* got to Kampala, the sun was completely awake and flexing its muscles. All the dew on spiderwebs and grass along the road had disappeared.

At the ministry building, a rusty brown gate was wide open next to a wooden sentry box large enough for only one person, marked SECURICO. It was empty. That perhaps was a good sign. In the parking lot, there were only two cars, huge SUV Pajeros with government license plates. The office building was beautiful: old and broad, with thick cement walls, and a veranda all around divided by tall, solid columns. It was the kind built in the colonial days, when the British could get all the materials and land they demanded, once they had ordered the local people to move away. There were huge windows all along the walls of the wide one-level building to let in cooling air. The walls were painted gray up to about hip level and white above. Or what was once white, Christine noted. It looked like the government was saving on painting expenses.

Christine walked around the building looking for an entrance. She saw a doorway at one corner. In she went and immediately found herself outside again in a courtyard: a large square plot of grass with small flowers, sunlight, and more office windows and doors facing onto it. How nice. Her workmate in D.C., Tamika, in their windowless office on the eighth floor of a building in the gray downtown, would envy her now. Christine peered into a window. Because of the blinding sunlight, she could only make out space, lots of it, and large, heavy-looking wooden furniture. What should she do? Ah, here. Was this the reception area? It was a corner room with a round wooden counter from wall to wall. A young woman, pregnant, or perhaps merely fat and ripe-looking, sat behind the counter. Her shiny red dress was stretched tight across her breasts and stomach. She was bent over a green piece of cloth she was embroidering. Christine recognized that particular harsh green Nytil Jinja cloth that was used to make chairbacks in many of the poorer homes. After many washings, by hand of course, the rough cotton became beautifully soft and faded into a pale guava-leaf green.

Christine stood there for a moment. The receptionist did not look up. Christine said, "Good morning." No reaction. She cleared her throat and raised her voice. "Good morning."

The receptionist looked up startled, then frowned. She turned back to finish a stitch and asked without looking up, "Can I help you?"

"I'd like to see Mr. Musozi."

The receptionist gave Christine a look that seemed to say, don't you know anything? "Mr. Musozi?" she asked.

Didn't she know who he was, for God's sake? "Yes, the Director of—"

"I know that. I work here." A pause. Two more stitches.

What to do? Should she have addressed the receptionist as "Auntie" like the market women did? "Well, can you direct me to his office?"

"Does he know you were coming?"

"Yes." Christine felt pricks of annoyance. But the less said, the better. Back in the States, she had got used to nonsensical road-blocks like this set up by receptionists, clerks, police, and sales-people who assumed that she didn't know what she wanted, who she was asking for, where she was or was supposed to be, and, of course, that she couldn't read a map. Not to mention those who couldn't or wouldn't understand her accent. So Christine had spoken slowly and loudly, but speaking more clearly, to her, meant hitting the consonants harder, which actually was less American and therefore less clear to Americans. After about two years she learned to slur a little, and then did so unconsciously after that. Now back here, at the airport, for example, she had slipped into her American accent, then stopped talking abruptly, mid-sentence, feeling foolish. Maama and Patti laughed, but the bag-gage clerk gave her a disparaging look, as if to say, you poor lost wanna-be-*mzungu*.

Anyway, who was this fat receptionist to interrogate her? Christine had liked her womanly pregnant good looks, but now was taken aback; she was so feminine and yet so hostile. More-over to a "sister," as was said back in the States, except that here the two of them were not sisters since everyone was black.

Finally, the receptionist said, "Mr. Musozi went to bury in the village. I don't think he will be here today." She seemed to smile maliciously, triumphantly at Christine.

Well, Christine hadn't been a "sistah" for nothing. "Miss, you *think*, or don't you know? Would it be too much to ask you to find out?" She put as much sarcasm as she could in her voice, and gestured toward a huge dusty black phone sitting on the counter like a gigantic dead beetle. It looked like a remnant from the colonial days that hadn't been used or dusted since then.

The receptionist ignored the phone. "Did he know his relative would die?"

"Don't ask me! Look, this shouldn't be so difficult—"

"Even if he was coming today, he wouldn't be here at this time. It's only nine o'clock. First, he has to take his children to school and his wife to work."

"Listen." Christine put both her hands on the counter firmly. "I am the new Executive Assistant to the Director of the Human Rights Commission. Mr. Musozi specifically asked me to come in today." She took a deep breath and then continued slowly, "Now, is there someone who can direct me to my office? Besides you, of course." Christine stepped back and waited.

Incredibly, the receptionist broke into a huge smile, put her sewing to the side, and stood up, straightening her tight dress over her bulging breasts and belly. "Eeeeh, why didn't you tell me? Christine Mugisha, yes? You are very, *very* welcome. My name is Peninah. Oo-oh, you are the lady Mr. Musozi has been praising. Okaaay. *Bambi*, how are you?" She held out both hands warmly, and Christine, confused, placed both of hers in them. The receptionist laughed, showing two neat rows of tiny white teeth and prominent purple-pink gums.

"I'm fine, thanks," Christine answered, not smiling. She took back her hands and crossed her arms in front of her chest.

"So, how was America?" Peninah asked enthusiastically, as if they were long-lost friends. "My uncle's wife, the second one, when he died, she went there with his two children. Stole them, I would say. It's been ten years now, can you imagine? And, you know, she had said she would help me go there to study catering, but have I heard anything?"

"Oh," Christine said and nodded. She couldn't believe what she was hearing. She deliberately looked at her watch. It was already after nine.

"*Bambi*, you got tired of the *bazungu*? Or weren't the dollars enough?" Peninah laughed at her own joke, while Christine watched her shaking breasts. The girl covered her mouth with fat brown fingers, each with startling white half-moon tips. She was beautiful, Christine admitted to herself grudgingly. She had large eyes with heavy "bedroom" eyelids, but almost no eyelashes or eyebrows. Pregnancy gave women such lush skin, as though they were now *really* women. She, Christine, had a stick figure with no hips or breasts to speak of, which had been more than okay in the States. But here, as her mother had reminded her already, as she piled more *matooke* onto her plate, it was not appreciated. People thought thin people had problems; one had best keep away, Maama said. Especially now with AIDS, *akawuka*—the little worm.

Peninah pulled up the counter opening and came out from behind it. "I will take you to Mr. Oduro. He works with Mr. Musozi on the Commission. Oh, there he is. Georgi!" she shouted at a tall, thin, very black man walking rapidly down the corridor. He stopped, turned, and stood stock still, looking down, not at them, as he waited. Peninah continued, "He is always the first one here. He eats and sleeps work." She shrugged her fat, soft-looking shoulders.

A real officer at last. Christine sighed with relief as they approached him. She reached out her hand. He shook it with a quick jerk, then dropped it without a smile, without any expression at all. He simply glanced at her then away, like a bird. "I'm Christine Mugisha, the new assis—"

"Yes. I know. Mr. Musozi had a death in the family. He will be here tomorrow. I'll show you your office. Thanks, Peninah." He turned like a stiff private and walked swiftly down the corridor. She followed at a trot as Peninah's languid laughter rose behind her. "Here. It leads into Mr. Musozi's office. He likes to talk when he works."

Mr. Oduro ushered her in, turned on his heel, and walked away. Just like that. The room was huge, with a bare table, chair, file cabinet, and bookshelf. There was the same kind of old-fashioned phone that the receptionist had. She wanted to ask if it worked but dared not. Mr. Oduro came back in with a large pile of dusty files and plunked then on her desk. Christine sneezed.

"You're allergic? Use Panadol. Every day. I don't even wash my shirts. They just get dirty again."

She stared at him in horror, then noticed his tight smile and laughed in relief. "Read these. Applications under the Human Rights Act. Mr. Musozi will explain. Ask Peninah for stationery. Call me Oduro." And he disappeared. Christine's eyes followed him. How odd, she thought. Well, he could make a joke, at least. Thank goodness Mr. Musozi had sounded congenial over the phone. And there was always Peninah for company. Oh, no! Christine smiled to herself.

She turned to the heap of files. The sun shone a big hot square of light right in the middle of her desk. Curtains, anyone? Hallo? But she didn't want to face Peninah again just yet. She should enjoy the sun after all those miserable winters dreaming about it. Dust danced in the light as Christine flicked through the files. She wanted to be ready and to impress Mr. Musozi tomorrow. There was nothing to distract her anyway; no e-mail or Internet. By the way, how on earth was she going to work without a computer? A sneeze punctuated her every thought. She should make a list of things she needed, including a writing pad and pen to make the list with!

Christine walked into Mr. Musozi's office to search for paper and pen. He had more furniture than she had, a worn carpet, more cabinets, and bookshelves overflowing with volumes of statutes, law journals, and more dusty files. His desk was strewn with paper that covered his computer, too. He had a picture of President Munino on the wall. A much younger, thinner Munino, just out of the "bush," when he had just taken power. The only other wall hanging was a government calendar with Munino's face again, more wealthy-looking now, less gaunt, more self-satisfied. Eight years later, eight years fatter, and he was still president. But he was better than anyone they'd had in the past: Idi Amin, Obote, and so on. A stable government and security in most of the country was a relief. People could breathe again. Christine hoped Munino wouldn't get a heart attack and die, what with all that weight. That would plunge Uganda back into chaos. Enough already.

Christine tore a piece of paper from a pad on Mr. Musozi's desk and found a pen underneath a pile of papers. Back in her office she wrote the list. She would give it to Peninah in the afternoon, not right now. No, not her again.

The sun was so brilliant the next morning, Christine wondered how she had woken up for eight years without it. She filled herself chock-full of antihistamines and coffee to ward off the accompanying sleepiness. Maama said her skirt was too short; she was taking too much medicine and too much coffee and she was going to be late. The traffic on the Entebbe-Kampala road was a mess these days. And by the way, did Christine have taxi fare? She should pack some lunch—

"Maama, stop! In case you've forgotten, I'm twenty-nine and have been living on my own—"

"I'm just warning you. Don't waste time, you better go now."

Christine sighed with exasperation and walked out. She would deal with Maama later. How on earth did Patti manage her?

Christine got to the office by eight-thirty. Oduro was already at his desk, and gave her a curt nod when she stopped by to say hallo. Feeling dismissed, she went back to her office. She was ready for Mr. Musozi. She had written down questions for him and organized the applications by date and category of request, valiantly ignoring the dust. She waited nervously, skimming through the files again. At about ten-thirty, she heard Peninah loudly welcome Mr. Musozi from across the courtyard. They talked for about twenty minutes. Christine checked her watch and wondered whether she should join them. Would that be rude or the polite thing to do? She hadn't worked long before she left Uganda, so was unsure about office etiquette here. Mr. Musozi had been nice on the phone, but still, he *was* the Director of the Human Rights Commission.

Mr. Musozi came in at last, bustling like a bumblebee. Christine was surprised to see that he was such a small man, but with a round ball of a belly sitting on his small frame. He looked pregnant. His gray suit was old, frayed, and out of shape, his glasses thick, old-fashioned large squares of brown plastic. If he didn't have a bald crown with short white fuzz around it, he could have been mistaken for a boy. A ripe and fertile schoolboy.

Christine nervously stood up to greet him. Mr. Musozi rushed over and grabbed her hand. "Hallo, hallo, hallo, welcome, Miss Mugisha, is it? Yes, yes, how are you? Good, good. I see you have settled in, straight to the paperwork, good, good."

He rushed to his office and sat down. His stream of words and energy swept though the air. "So, yes, yes, sorry about yesterday, had to go bury my *senga*, you know how people die. Every three months it seems I make the trip to Mubende, you have to, you know, or they will talk, and your wife will stop talking to you, and so on, and who will attend yours, you know? Yes, yes, our wonderful traditions, oh yes. Let's see, here we are, this is the Commission." He spread his short arms wide, showing her the two rooms. "The Uganda Human Rights Commission, set up by an Act of Parliament. Ha! Not what you were expecting, no?" He laughed cheekily, as if he had played a clever trick on her. Christine sat down, stunned.

"Now, now, where are we? What do you need to know? Let me bring you up to date. Our problem is money. Not surprised, eh? No, no, me neither." As he talked, he stood up, walked around his desk, drew out of his trouser pocket a large, startlingly white handkerchief, cleaned his glasses, folded the hanky in half, wiped his face, walked back to his seat, sat down, got back up again. Christine just sat there, mentally openmouthed.

Mr. Musozi stopped when Oduro walked in and shook hands with him. "Sorry about the loss."

"Yes, yes, these things happen. My mother's younger sister, you know? Well, she's gone, she's gone. And how is Karamoja? How is the project going?"

"Slow. I'm still trying to get the funds from Accounts to travel there. I can't do anything until I have been to the area and talked to the chiefs themselves."

"Yes, yes, the fight with Accounts, those thieves. Always the first step. Can't they at least give you half? Let them steal the rest." They both gave a short laugh. Mr. Musozi turned to Christine. "I hope you took this course back in America, 'How to Fight for Your Money.' It is required. Absolutely mandatory. You didn't? Well, that's the main thing we do here. Yes, yes." The two men laughed again. "Luckily you came with your own money. Very wise. Very wise indeed."

"Accounts won't like that," Oduro noted dryly, and they chuckled.

Christine didn't think it was so funny. This was exactly the kind of thing that made the most well-planned projects fail, the lack of money to implement them. If the money was allotted for the project, how dare the Accounts Department not release it? All of it. Not to mention the wasted time and energy begging. Such major setbacks should be dealt with, not laughed at! She couldn't stop herself: "Sir, why hasn't the Accounts Department been held—"

"Oh, no, no, my dear, do not call me sir, no, no, no. Just Musozi, okay?"

Before she could go on, an officer came in, then another and another, all to offer their condolences to Mr. Musozi. Christine went back to her desk after a few minutes, since it was clear his colleagues had settled down for a good talk. But she couldn't do very much before conferring with Mr. Musozi. The other officers passed back and forth by her desk, and her boss's high-pitched voice and squeal of laughter carried over to her room.

Was it the coffee that was making her tremble or was it frustration? Was she this nervous? Meanwhile, there was a party in full swing next door! Right away a major issue had cropped up: Accounts. How would she deal with that? Christine wanted to leave, to step out for some fresh air, but what would Musozi think? Should she tell him? She sensed something . . . sharp, perhaps, underneath his cheeky laughter. She ran her hands over her bare desk. They came away grimy. Another item for Peninah. Her boss must be very popular, or was it normal to spend half the morning chatting? She had forgotten how important, and to her mind silly, not to mention inefficient, courtesy was. God forbid the bereaved person might think you had a malicious reason for not expressing your sympathy. And a phrase or two wasn't enough; you had to listen to the story of the death and how the burial went while murmuring condolences: *"Nga kitalo, bambi"* and "We'll pray for you." Christine sat there looking out of her curtainless window blankly, then aimlessly flicked through the files she had studied already. How helpless she felt, how useless. How out of place.

By the time Musozi's visitors left, more than half the morning was gone. Musozi called her back into his office. At the same time an older woman in a faded *bussuti* of cream and blue flowers came in with a tray and two cups of tea. She placed the tea on Musozi's desk, then knelt down and greeted him in the lengthy Luganda way, with lots of questions, pauses, and sighs. She asked after his wife, the children, the other relatives, the farm, cows, and groundnuts. And then, of course, came the condolences. Christine wondered why Musozi let the old woman kneel through all that. In the office! Her hair was cut very short and smooth over her perfectly round head and it shone with oil. He called her Nnalongo—the mother of twins. She was too humble for Christine's taste. This wasn't the village! By the time they got to the tea, it was lukewarm. Nnalongo had already put in the sugar. It was so sickeningly sweet, Christine could not take more than two sips. Nnalongo asked them what they would have for lunch. Musozi repeated the question in English.

"I didn't know we got lunch here. And by the way, I know Luganda." She smiled to soften her rebuke.

"Some people forget, or try to. You people who go abroad,

165 ❧

you come back with all sorts of airs. My nephews too!" He laughed. "Nnalongo makes lunch and sells it here. She's a good cook. Isn't it true, *Nyabo?*"

"I try." Nnalongo smiled self-effacingly.

"I'll have *matooke* and meat. You should have the same, Christine. It's good."

"I don't eat meat."

Musozi stopped fidgeting with the papers on the desk and looked at her in astonishment. So did Nnalongo from her position on the floor. Then he said, "Oh, you're allergic? That's too bad."

"No."

"It's not Lent, is it? I can't keep up with these religious dates. Anyway, nothing can make me give up meat!" he patted his belly and laughed.

"It's for ethical reasons." Christine felt she should explain, in case he thought she had simply rejected his offer.

He stopped mid–face wipe. "What?"

"Well, um, cows and other animals are living beings that . . . that love their lives, and . . ." Musozi's incredulous expression deepened. He took off his glasses and peered more closely at her as he cleaned them, as if the answer was in her face. ". . . And these animals are killed in such inhumane ways . . ."

"Inhumane?" He burst out laughing, then turned to Nnalongo. "You heard what she said?" He translated: "She said animals are not killed the way people are." He whipped out his handkerchief and wiped his face as if to control his laughter. "Let's not talk about how *people* are killed!" He laughed harder.

Nnalongo laughed softly behind her hand, then asked, "And goats? Sheep? Fish too?"

"Well, actually, I eat fish, because, because . . ." How could she explain this? Where should she start?

Nnalongo said, slowly and emphatically, as if to an idiot child, "Animals are not people."

"I *know*, but . . . but—"

Musozi swept away her attempt with a wave of his handkerchief. "Give her beans, like a commoner. Maybe she ate enough meat in America. Yes, yes, that must be it."

Christine knew he didn't mean to insult her, but she felt insulted all the same, and annoyed at not being able to explain the obvious. Annoyed at looking like a fool on the very first day. Annoyed at everybody's constant laughter. Nnalongo got up from the floor and left, still smiling.

Musozi asked, "How long were you in the States?"

"Eight years."

"Too long, too long. That's why. You'll settle in soon, don't worry. Yes, yes. You'll like meat again. When you feel lucky to get it."

The standard vegetarian speech was silly in response to that. Or was it silly, period? Was it just a matter of time before she would cave in, settle down, become herself again, as Musozi would call it? Whatever that self was. Her American voice, disgusted, silently replied, *whatever*.

The beans were terrible. They reminded Christine of the meals she ate almost every day for six years during her high school days at Gayaza, a government boarding school. She remembered weevils floating dead in the muddy brown water that went for bean soup. You could not avoid crunching into one or two of the weevils as you gobbled down your food in twenty minutes or less. At least these beans didn't have weevils, but she tasted the memory, made more immediate by the same farty bean smell, and lost her appetite. Back then, Christine had vowed never to go hungry again. Ever. "By any means necessary," she had written in capital letters in her diary, quoting her hero of that week, Malcolm X. Now she chose to eat beans. Very funny.

Christine was so glad to leave work that day. Nothing much was accomplished that afternoon either because Mr. Musozi was called to an urgent meeting. As he rushed out, he slammed another bulging file onto her desk, saying, "Here you go: some more meat to chew on." He chuckled. "The best way to start is to dive right in. Get involved. Let's talk tomorrow," and he swept out, wiping his face and smiling hugely.

At the taxi park, the jostling hawkers, crying babies, and jangling music mirrored the turmoil in her mind. She wasn't able to read during the *matatu* ride back to Entebbe. There was a lot to untangle, to make sense of, including why on earth she was so troubled. She was home, right? She felt as if she had to make some sort of a decision, but about what? She couldn't turn around and leave, just like that. Go back to the States with her tail between her legs. Then what? This was ridiculous; she didn't have to leave. She pressed her eyes closed to keep the tears back.

The taxi's tumble and drone calmed Christine down somewhat. She looked forward to a peaceful tea with Maama and Patti. Her sister worked as an administrator for a Christian organization for the disabled, also in Kampala. Christine wondered why Patti had not left home and moved to the capital, but was also glad she hadn't. Almost all of Maama's letters praised Patti for one thing or another. At least Patti is here keeping me company, she wrote. You know I'm growing old. Patti reminds me to take my insulin, she drives me to Kampala and the village now that my eyesight is going. I'm so glad she's here. *Come back,* was what Christine heard.

She was free to live wherever she wanted to, of course. But, repeating this to herself didn't relieve the weight of guilt. A dutiful daughter should be at her old parents' side, just as Maama had looked after her own mother, and Taata's mother too, before they passed away. Well, here Christine was, back home again, wasn't she? Moreover, she found Maama just as strong and resolute as ever, she wasn't an invalid at all. Maama and Patti now looked after a cousin's twin daughters. Both parents had died. The girls, Nyakato and Kengoma, filled the house with laughter and young voices again, which renewed Maama's energy. So, actually, there had been nothing to worry about at all.

The taxi entered Entebbe's fresh, lake-filled air as the evening mellowed. The sun's last rays seemed to mark the end of that day's possibilities. Christine could not help noticing, again, what had been so ordinary years before. For example, there were no bus stops; passengers called out to the driver, *"Awo, Ssebo, ku taala."* "Right there, sir, at the light," or "by the big mango tree," or *"ku Leeké,"* meaning Lake Victoria Hotel, which was opposite the golf course that had now become a pasture for cows. As passengers scrambled off the taxi one by one, it got lighter and rattled even more noisily. Christine had not realized that she had stored the sensations deep inside, all the small details that made up the theater of the everyday. The memories now rose up and resonated with the reality around her. The way the conductor, a teenage boy with bloodshot eyes (from either too much sun or a drinking habit, already) collected, meticulously arranged, and folded dirty blue, yellow, and brown notes in one hand while maneuvering, half bent, between the tight passenger seats. The oddly familiar whiff of sweat from the boy's armpit as he reached over her head. The sound of the *matatu* door heaving open and clanging shut repeatedly. Yes, that was exactly how the heavy creaking doors had sounded way back when. That was the true sound of home. Or was it? What about the changes that did not match her memories?

Christine's stop was at Queens Road. She raised her voice. *"Awo, ku Queenzi."* She forced herself to pronounce "Queens" in what she and her sisters had called a *maalo*, village-ish, back when they were kids. But it wasn't just a different pronunciation; it had become a *kiganda* word, like how money was *esente*, from the word "cent." If she pronounced "Queens" properly, the driver wouldn't understand, or would refuse to understand what to him was an affected way of speaking. She, luckily or not, had been to a "good" school, where she had been taught to speak English properly, that is, like an Englishman, which, of course, was impossible for her to do. Not that the English themselves spoke their language in one "proper" way. Nor was it theirs alone anymore. English was no one's and everyone's now. Or so the unloved step-children to the English tribe insisted. Oh, what tangled webs we weave. Christine smiled. Wrong quote, wrongly quoted! The words and accents in all their wrongness and rightness were the sounds of home. They made sense here, and she understood how, in a way no foreigner could.

Christine walked for about ten minutes down Queens Road to her mother's house. The residential area had been built for colonial administrators around the 1940s. "Entebbe" meant "chair" in Luganda; the town was the seat of the colonial government. At independence, the capital was moved to Kampala. Entebbe remained a small, intimate town with a few ministries left, an international airport, the half-empty National Zoo, and the surrounding lakeside villages of fishermen. The colonial houses were now occupied by civil servants like her mother had been. They were now allowed to buy the spacious bungalows. Christine was so glad Maama had remained in town instead of retiring to the village, Rusozi, in western Uganda. That was considered the family's real home because it was where Taata was born and grew up, although his family had migrated from the west, somewhere in or near Congo, long before the present borders existed. Maama was a Munyoro from Masindi. The question rose up and faced Christine again: Where was home, then, really? Luckily, her family had grown to love Entebbe, its cozy size, its lack of hustle and bustle, and the blue expanse of lake all around it like a shield.

The walk through the long evening shadows calmed Christine down. Maybe work hadn't been that bad. Surely she would adjust, get used to it. It wasn't a matter of her becoming like them (them who?) or they more like her. She couldn't be that different. She sighed. The dusty road, still not repaired since she had left, was the familiar, imperfect, potholed rut.

At home, Maama was having tea in the living room and reading the day's newspapers. She had her glasses on, which had been another surprise for Christine. It was a mark of time passing, and of Maama's coming frailty, however strong she was now. The glasses were perched low on Maama's wide nose, the same nose Christine now saw in her own mirror every morning. Her toes and fingers were just like Patti's. Perhaps they were simply different copies of one another. Looking at her mother, so at home in the familiar room, Christine wanted to kiss her in greeting, but they didn't do that. It was too *zungu.*

Maama looked up. "You're back. How was it?"

"Okay, I guess."

Maama lifted her glasses off her eyes and tilted her head in question. Christine sat down hard on the sofa and sighed heavily. "Frankly, work was a mess. We did absolutely *nothing* today."

"It's only the first day—"

"I know, but I thought at least they would be ready for me, you know, have a computer on my desk, for Christ's sake."

"This isn't America." Maama smiled.

Christine gave her an irritated look, but went on. "And then there's this receptionist, Peninah, who's going to give me trouble, I just know it."

Maama smiled sympathetically and took a sip from her flowered china teacup. "Be patient. You're always so quick to judge."

"Oh yes, blame me."

Maama shrugged and put her glasses back on.

"We've been planning my arrival for months!"

"You know how it is here."

Her mother paused, as if silence would ease Christine's exasperation, then offered in a softer voice, "Tea?"

Maama's sympathy irritated Christine even more. "Yeah, tea will solve all our problems." She noisily turned her teacup over, banged it down onto its saucer, filled it with steaming tea, and put the pot down onto the tray as hard as she could. Maama looked at her for a long moment, then turned back to the paper. Christine sipped her tea, fuming. How did Maama do it? She turned her into a silly, petulant child all over again.

As Christine poured herself another cup, Maama exclaimed, "Oh, look, Lisa's wedding announcement! Your friend Lisa Atwoki from your Gayaza days, remember?"

"Of course. Who is she marrying?"

"Dr. Leopold Musiime. He must be the Musiime who heads Nsambya Hospital."

"Isn't he a little old?"

"Not for your age. Lisa is also almost thirty, isn't she? People have been getting married right and left. You've missed. And they all have asked about you."

"About what? Whether I'm married or not, right? When I was coming back."

Maama gave her a long questioning look, then turned her eyes back to the paper. Her body was still, alert. "Is that a bad question to ask?"

"Prying into my business," Christine muttered. Why was she acting so defensive? She should just shut up. Be nice. She drank the rest of her tea in silence.

Maama turned a page of her paper, and as she scanned it, murmured, "I had been wondering about that."

"What?"

"Calm down, Christine. I have just been wondering, that's all—whenever people ask."

"If you want to ask me, ask." Christine gave a sharp laugh of annoyance.

"Christine, you get angry for no good reason, just like Taata. A normal person would want to get married, have kids; it's not such a strange question. The house is so lively now with Kemigisha's children."

"Especially since Rosa passed away and I and Patti are not getting you grandkids." Christine snorted. Her scalp began to itch. She scratched it fiercely.

"How can you say that! All these things are in God's hands. And don't scratch your head like that; you'll go bald." Maama softened her voice. "Christine, maybe if you were with someone you'd be happier."

Christine shot up off the sofa. "What do you mean *happier*? Like you were?" She stomped out of the room, ignoring her mother's shocked call.

Christine hurried outside, out of Maama's reach and expectations. Happier? Happier? Okay then, she was abnormal. She had come back, hadn't she? What more did Maama want? She was only twenty-nine! What her mother didn't know was that Christine had been forced to begin her life all over again when she arrived in America. She had to learn everything anew; even roads were crossed differently over there. No wonder she had felt young, foolish even, for years. Now, back here, she was instantly an old maid! It was ludicrous. She laughed angrily and kicked at the road's loose stones.

All the same, she shouldn't have answered Maama like that. Christine never would have before, of course. She had forgotten how strong and indirect and persistent Maama was. A bully, really. No, that wasn't fair. How on earth had she thought she could live at home with her? Back in the States, after a hard day of fake smiles and isolation, alone in her apartment at night, Christine had imagined the three of them, with Patti, as close companions growing older together; serenely sipping tea or shelling a large basket of fresh peas, smiling. The proverbial strong African family. She laughed out loud again in the fading light. The dream itself *was* home. Then what was this? Home was supposed to be a permanent, solid fact. A created one was fake, wasn't it?

Christine walked around the house to the back, where she found Patti working in the vegetable garden. The green leaves of the banana trees were streaked with yellow, now that it was the dry season, and the maize plants were sand-colored. Patti was bent over, picking bean pods from the short plants. Her open basket was almost full. She turned and squinted through the evening light as Christine walked up.

"Hard at work, as usual."

"I had to get to these before the insects did. They're ready."

Patti continued picking the pods and throwing them into her basket. Christine stood apart, careful not to soil her shoes, as she watched her sister's rhythmic movements.

Patti stopped and turned. "What's wrong? I know you didn't come to help me." They smiled. Patti knew her too well.

Christine sighed and looked away. "It's Maama. She's been harassing me about marriage again."

Patti grinned as she continued working. "Well, you know, she wants us to be settled. To be happy."

"Please! I've come back here; isn't that enough for her? I'm sick of being told—"

"Christine, you know you can do what you want." Patti straightened up and sighed. "Anyway, what you want and what Maama wants aren't so different. In fact, if anything, you've become more like her. I live with her, I know—"

"I really don't know how you manage it, Patti, really."

"It's my home." She wiped small beads of sweat off her forehead with one hand and waved at the garden with the other. "I've worked on this soil for years. Not that there is a difference." She gave a half-laugh.

Christine shrugged, but was reminded of what Mr. Musozi had said as he gave her another file this afternoon. Dive in. Get involved.

Patti looked at Christine sympathetically for a long, quiet moment. "It'll be all right." She touched Christine's arm gently. "I'm kind of tired. I'm going in."

"Okay. Me too. Soon," Christine answered.

Left alone, Christine walked up to the highest point of Queens

Road and turned back west. The sun had disappeared, but the sky still glowed red, pink, and purple. The lake far away gleamed flat and placid. Most of the compounds now had less lawn and more vegetable garden. The extravagant leaves and vines became huge dark shapes in the dimming light. Christine had to admit she loved these disorganized gardens where life unleashed itself every which way. They were the exact opposite of the tiny rectangular patches of immaculate green lawns back in the States that had to be watered, fertilized, fenced off, teased, and begged to grow. One day, all this vibrancy, this living chaos, would be normal again. One day. But this meant she wouldn't notice it anymore.

The dark was closing in. Christine could hardly see now as the last blood-red streaks across the sky turned indigo. She sighed deeply. Patti and her boss were right. She should dig deep down into this mud with her bare hands until she couldn't remove it from her fingernails. Merge with it, like day had smoothly become its opposite, night. Christine sat on a huge stone between the road and a garden. The words she had heard the whole day were like that too: *Queenzi*, *Leeke*, *cente*, and so on. A new language formed by old ones running underneath and over one another. An ever-changing in-between. Christine could accept this fluidity as she now accepted the night creeping up over her, this blanket of warm dusk. And not just because it was inevitable, but because it was different every night: a performance, an adventure. She would have to learn all over again how to live in this new old place called home. The sky was now completely black. And somewhere far away, right now, it was dawn.

A NOTE ABOUT THE AUTHOR

Doreen Baingana is from Uganda and lives in the United States. She has a law degree from Makerere University, Kampala, and an M.F.A. from the University of Maryland. She has won the Washington Independent Writers Fiction prize, been a finalist for the Caine Prize in African Writing, and received an Artist Grant from the District of Columbia Commission of the Arts and Humanities.

READING GROUP COMPANION:

TROPICAL FISH

Tropical Fish details the coming of age of three sisters after the fall of the Idi Amin regime in Uganda. The questions that follow are meant to spark discussion about the impact of politics, faith, and culture on their progress to adulthood, as well as debate on what it truly means to be at home.

THE GUIDE

1. Discuss the stereotypes you associate with Africa and Africans. How does Baingana shatter and/or reinforce those images and ideas in the stories that comprise *Tropical Fish*?

2. In many coming-of-age stories, the main focus is on establishing identity and a sense of belonging. How do Christine, Patti, and Rosa "come of age" throughout the collection? What are the

markers of their developing sense of self? Which of the sisters resonates with you the most? Do you find them likable?

3. Discuss the battle between traditional African religion (juju) and the influence of Christianity that is woven throughout the collection. How does Baingana illustrate each as an influential force in the Mugisha household? How do both strands of belief affect the development of the three sisters?

4. In the story "Tropical Fish," Baingana writes: "The Nile perch is ugly and tasteless, but it is huge, and provides a lot more food for the populace. But it was eating up all the smaller, rarer, gloriously colored tropical fish. Many of these rare species were not named, let alone discovered, before they disappeared. Every day, somewhere deep and dark, it was too late." (p. 109)

How does this passage encapsulate the political and economic state of Uganda as presented throughout the collection? How does it represent Christine's relationship with Peter and her own feelings about herself? And with regard to the rest of the collection, how does it underscore the sisters' relationships with people outside their immediate family?

5. In "A Thank-You Note," Baingana humanizes and personalizes the AIDS crisis in Africa. Did you find anything startling

about Rosa's voice in this story? If so, what? How does this story globalize notions of sexuality? How does the author use the exuberance of youth to underscore the nature of the epidemic?

6. Christine's childlike wonder at the relationship between her parents in "Green Stones" is gradually brought down to earth with the revelation of infidelity and alcoholism. What are your feelings about Maama's decision to stick by her husband through it all? How does her relationship with Taata shape her life without him and her relationship with her daughters? What does his death instill in Maama?

7. In "Hunger," Patti's relationships with God and her peers are severely tested. How does her inner voice (her diary voice) differ from her actions? Do you find her to be long-suffering or a complainer? How does she doubt herself and her sense of belonging at the Gayaza High School? Do you believe she is truly at peace after her experience at the fellowship meeting?

8. How do Christine's feelings about home evolve over the course of the stories? Compare her decision to explore the Western world to Patti's decision to remain at home. Of the two sisters, who do you believe is more at home with herself by the collection's end?

9. How does Christine's experience of racism in Los Angeles and Washington differ from her experience in Uganda? What are the similarities? How does Ugandan culture inform her experiences abroad? How does leaving Uganda and becoming more immersed in American culture affect her relationships with other Ugandans? What lessons does she take back to Uganda with her? Do you think she is an idealist at heart?